Happy
Reading!

— Liam

OFF SCOT FREE

OFF SCOT FREE

Liam Ashe

KNAVE

Off Scot Free

Copyright © 2023 William Oscar Ashe

www.liamashe.com

All rights reserved. No portion of this book may be reproduced in any form without permission from the publisher, except as permitted by U.S. copyright law. For permissions contact info@knavepublishing.com.

First Printing, September 2023

ISBN 978-1-7346854-9-7

This is a work of fiction. Names, characters, businesses, places, events, locales, and incidents are either the products of the author's imagination or used in a fictitious manner. Any resemblance to actual persons, living or dead, or actual events is purely coincidental.

Knave Publishing
821 Herndon Ave #141226
Orlando, FL 32803

www.knavepublishing.com

For Jeff,
my rock and my light

Elle Cunningham Mackay Mysteries

Thou Shalt Not Kilt
Off Scot Free

Prologue

The lanky young man took a tentative step through the open gate. He scratched his chin with one hand and continued into the empty security yard. On either side of the gap, razor-wire-topped fencing stretched into the darkness. A feeble pool of light spilled from the lone fixture, illuminating the dirt around him. Above, the moonless North Carolina night sky revealed nothing. He looked to his left and right and shrugged.

"Hmmm," he muttered. "No parade." The gate, now well behind him, replied with the clack of a lock.

Even in the dim light, it was clear that his clothes were stained and several sizes too big. Untied laces trailed behind his worn shoes. Hollow eyes and a few days of patchy beard made him look several years older than the twenty-five he had earned. A flash of lightning lit the sky to the south as the first few drops of rain pricked the back of his neck. As he stood in the slowly strengthening rain, his movements were measured and deliberate.

In one hand, Duncan Scott held a cardboard box with his name hand-printed in large, blocky letters. He removed the top, letting it fall to the ground. From the jumbled contents, he withdrew a faded photograph of three young girls mugging for an unseen camera. The trio wore out-of-fashion bathing suits and straw hats; one sported oversized sunglasses. Behind them, a tall black-and-white lighthouse split the pale blue sky.

Despite the age of the image, the red hair of the smallest girl blazed like embers. From the distant past, her eyes regarded him with a mix of sadness and warmth. Duncan shook his head and used his sleeve to wipe away a tear.

"Time to find the truth," he promised himself.

He discarded the open box, spilling its contents onto the dirt yard. Dabbing a few stray raindrops from the surface of the photo, he carefully tucked it into his inside shirt pocket.

Duncan stepped from the circle of light and into the night. The state lockup fell behind him as he plodded his way down the road to St. Andrews. With only nine, perhaps ten, miles to go, he pulled up his collar while the rain began to pour down in earnest.

1

A day to come seems longer than a year that's gone.

— Scottish Proverb

In retrospect, Elle should have seen it coming. As the afternoon gave way to evening, the sky through the arched window had dimmed from blue to red to starless black. For two hours, she had focused, uninterrupted, on the reams of research neatly positioned around her on the floor. Sitting with legs crossed in the center of her sister's study, her back to the door, she was vulnerable.

Dulled by an endless trickle of names, dates, and statistics, Elle never registered footfalls muffled by thick carpeting. A sturdy arm wrapped around her neck, pulling her back. Robbed of her balance, she was an easy target. A second assailant jabbed her right side with something sharp, rigid, and iridescent.

Caught off guard for only a second, Elle curled her body forward into a defensive position. With her unsecured left hand, she reached behind her, exploring one attacker for any vulnerable spot. Her fingers found an exposed rib cage.

Her search was rewarded with a cascade of giggles. The arm around her neck released its loose choke hold, and the small body behind her collapsed to the floor. Elle let herself fall backward, gently pinning her niece to the carpet. The giggles continued. As she lay back, the other twin came into Elle's view, standing over her with a sparkling plastic wand clutched in his hand. He poked her in the side again and made an ominous whooshing sound between pursed lips.

"No fair," he said. "I froze you. You can't move. No fair."

Elle obliged and contracted her face into a motionless mask of despair. Beneath her, the giggling sputtered and stopped.

"Aunt Elle, I'm stuck," the girl said. "Get up, get up, get up."

"Sorry, Izzy. Can't. Move. Frozen."

"Simon, make her stop. Un-froze her," the girl demanded, lapsing back into giggles.

Simon shrugged and jabbed his aunt once again with the wand. Elle made a show of fighting the enchantment.

"Not. Working. Powerful. Magic. Stuck. Forever."

Izzy started to protest, but her words surrendered to laughter. Simon looked at the wand, shook it once, and lost interest. The four-year-old dropped the toy at Elle's side and wandered from the room.

"Baby girl, I held them off as long as I could." Elle's sister's voice came from the open doorway. "You sure you're going to be all right tonight? Sophie wants to be home before ten, so we won't be gone more than an hour or two."

From her position on the floor, Elle waved her off. "I think we're good. I found a comfy spot. Might just lie here all night." Her makeshift pillow began to giggle again, bobbing Elle's head back and forth.

"Sounds like fun," Lana replied with a soft Carolina twang. "And if you see Izzy, tell her there's ice cream in the garage freezer. Chocolate or butter pecan, but only one scoop. She has to pick one or the other."

"Mama, I'm right here." Elle felt her niece's arms and legs flail for attention. Unable to win against the promise of ice cream, Elle sat up, releasing the prisoner.

"Isabella Rachel Cunningham-Klein, where did you come from?" her mother asked with mock astonishment.

"Magic?" Izzy suggested. Without waiting for an answer, the young girl ran after her brother, her mind focused on dessert.

"Thanks again for watching them tonight." Lana straightened the cowl on her dress in the hall mirror. "We haven't had a date night in weeks."

"You look fine. Actually, better than fine," Elle added, then let out a long, slow sigh. "How'd you get all the tall genes?"

From her low perspective, Elle thought her sister resembled the impossibly graceful, well-dressed offspring of a giraffe and a gazelle. Lana was tall and lean, with just enough curve to coax the plaid-with-emerald-green sweater dress into accentuating her shape.

"Just lucky, I guess. Don't know how, though. As short as Mama is, from all the pictures it never looked like Daddy was any taller."

"Love the dress. Don't recognize the tartan, though."

"I don't know that it is one. May be just a plaid. Got it on sale at Blue Water," Lana admitted. "All I know is that it's warm. I'm going to be standing for an hour in that big, drafty hall. Everyone in their great kilts and wool jackets, the thermostat will be on sub-arctic. It's a good compromise between going full-on Scottish and freezing to death."

"Well, you look amazing."

Only twenty-four months apart, the two women had the same eye-catching red hair. Lana's, however, enjoyed the benefit of a gifted stylist and world-class colorist. The modified pixie cut sported a touch of tousled length on top. To Elle, it made her older sister somehow look both more tomboyish and more strikingly feminine at the same time. Elle, on the other hand, had settled for a scrunchie.

At the compliment, Lana turned to her sister and gave a dazzling smile. "Love you, baby girl."

From somewhere past the hall, Sophie's voice called out, "Lana, car's here. Let's go."

"One sec." Lana offered Elle a hand. She gave her little sister a quick hug as her wife appeared in the doorway. Shorter than Lana by four or five inches, Sophie cultivated a more conservative style. A little black dress perfectly offset her long chestnut brown hair. A vintage sequined shrug added a little flash—but only a little. In both fashion and most conversations, Sophie was content to let Lana do the heavy lifting.

Elle reached out and smoothed a wrinkle from Sophie's collar. Her sister-in-law responded with a warm hug.

"Elle, you are my hero," she said. "You have no idea how much I appreciate this."

"Are you kidding? You all have been putting up with me for more than a month now. It's the least I can do. Angus and I will watch the twins; you guys have a blast at the cèilidh."

"We will probably just stay an hour, then maybe a drink at the bar at the Portnoy," Sophie replied. "This get-up took a lot of effort, so I've got to show it off while I can." A message on Sophie's phone pinged. "The car's waiting; we better go."

A few moments later, the front door opened and closed as the couple left for the evening. Somewhere deep in the house, Elle's basset hound howled a belated warning.

On the den's television, a pair of actors in bad wigs attempted a lover's quarrel. Their accents suited a high school production of *A Streetcar Named Desire*. A woman's voice narrated the scene with a heavy nasal emphasis on each salacious detail. "Two years after falling *in* love, the pair had a falling *out*. But in the case of Harold Jenkins, was it a fall or was he pushed?"

"Totally pushed," Elle said to the empty room. "Otherwise, why would this be on TV?"

Splayed across her lap, Angus the basset hound chuffed, his lips flapping slightly. He rolled his body to one side, exposing his neck. Elle rewarded his effort with a slow scratch under the chin.

Her full attention given to the dog's comfort, she almost missed the snap, or maybe a click, that sounded just beyond the patio doors. It was a subtle disturbance, but enough to prick the back of her neck. Elle found the remote buried under one of Angus' ears and hit pause. Sliding the lounging hound to the next cushion, she turned in a slow, deliberate rotation to check the patio for signs of movement. The tree-covered deck was, as usual, unlit and further obscured by a moonless night and sheer white curtains draping the doors.

She rose and stepped to the side of the French doors, careful not to disturb the filmy fabric. For a moment, she stood, motionless, her eyes searching for any telltale hint of an intruder. Never letting her gaze move from the darkness, Elle's left hand felt along the wall for the outdoor light switch. Her fingers in place, she took a deep breath and flipped the switch.

The patio just out of her sight was bathed in a halo of landscaping lights and strung market lanterns. In the center of the deck, a small figure stood, frozen and illuminated, dressed in a dark jacket, matching pants, and an oversized leather bag. The breath rushed from Elle's lungs in an audible whoosh as she unlocked and threw open the patio door.

"What the living hell are you doing creeping around out there in the dark?"

"Language, young lady," her mother replied with a shake of her head.

"You scared the life out of me."

"Can't a mother stop by unannounced to see her favorite daughter?"

"Mama, Lana's at the cèilidh."

"Ellie, that's not nice. You are both my favorites, outside of your language, of course."

"Of course." Elle crossed her arms in feigned disappointment, never moving from her spot in the doorway.

"God was very good to me and blessed me with two very different daughters to love. Few mothers are that lucky." Vee Cunningham stared at her daughter for a moment in silence. With an affected deference, she added, "Have I groveled enough to come inside? Or should I just sit here in the cold?"

"And the dark. And the rain. Don't forget the rain," Elle replied as she clicked off the patio lights. She stepped back from the door and ushered her mother into the den.

"Mama, you really shouldn't be tippy-toeing around out there without warning. Why not knock or call?"

"The lights are off in the twins' room, and I didn't want to wake them. Such little angels, but they aren't the easiest to put to bed. Honestly, I'm impressed. It's eleven, and they are already asleep. What hoodoo did you use on them?"

"Don't judge me, but they each got two scoops of ice cream and a pinky swear not to tell their moms."

Vee laughed and settled into a chair across from the sofa as Elle returned to her spot next to Angus. "Ellie, it's the only thing that works. I've been giving them two scoops for months."

It was Elle's turn to laugh. "Lana is going to love hearing about that! Our perfect, law-abiding mother bribing her grandchildren with illicit desserts. Scandal."

The older woman leaned forward and winked at her daughter. "My dear, you can't tell on me without ratting yourself out, too. These things only work if all us ne'er-do-wells stick together."

Her mother's good spirits always brought out the best in Elle's mood. Although known across Eagle Island as a shrewd businesswoman and savvy entrepreneur, Vee Cunningham was gifted with an impish nature Elle found infectious. Beneath that grandmotherly exterior, Elle's mother always seemed to clutch a giddy secret with both hands—she was forever on the brink of getting away with *something*. Elle learned long ago that she was never as successful as her mother at either keeping a secret or getting away with the mischief she caused.

Still, Elle reasoned, she and her sister had inherited their mother's dry wit and sharp mind. This was usually—though not always—enough to get Elle out of the trouble she attracted like a lodestone.

Elle leaned forward to meet her mother halfway and planted a gentle kiss on the older woman's forehead. "Still, I don't like you walking around this late at night."

Vee lifted her purse from beside the chair and set it firmly in her lap. She patted the side of the bag. "Ellie, I've got my protection with me at all times."

Elle shuddered; she didn't want to have this conversation again. "Mama, you know how much I hate guns. Always have. Especially with children in the house, it just doesn't feel safe."

"Well, I've got my CCH permit, the safety is on, and my carry purse stays locked when I'm in the house. Plus, it's not like that guard dog of yours is doing much good." Angus began to snore. Vee glanced at the frozen frame on the television. "And you've been bingeing too many of these murder TV shows. Please tell me you don't let Izzy and Simon watch this trash."

"Before bed, it's two mind-numbing hours of *Sunny Side Station. Operation Cold Case* is strictly after lights out."

"So, who's done gone and done who wrong this week?" her mother asked with what Elle suspected was more than feigned interest. In the four decades since she had emigrated from Scotland to the North Carolina coast, Vee had worked diligently to scrub her soft, lyrical Shetland accent with its touches of Scandinavian lilt. In its place, she had hobbled together a patchwork quilt of Southern affectations to a passable Midwestern base.

"An unhappily married couple in Memphis. The husband was shot by the pistol he kept *securely* in his nightstand." She glanced at Vee's purse, then shot her mother a dirty look. "No one else could have done it. The wife's cell phone, however, shows she was driving home two counties away, and her sister was at a bar not far from the wife. The wife's jealous boyfriend was in lock-up."

"So sad," Vee replied with a shake of her head. "Someone will get away with murder."

"Hmmm, not so fast. I think that if they check the wife's cell phone and trace the sister's route, they are going to line up. Probably just gave her sister her phone, the sister is seen at the bar, and they both are alibied. Meanwhile, she's hightailing back roads to make it to her house, kill her husband, and rush back to get her phone and continue on home."

Vee sat, open-mouthed, and raised both hands in surrender. "Ellie, you missed your calling as a detective. Or prosecutor. Or interrogation specialist with the CIA. Or Spanish inquisitor."

Her train of thought was interrupted by the front door chime. "Mama?" Lana's voice called from the front hall.

"In here with Ellie," she called back. Lana and Sophie turned the corner from the hall and dropped their wraps on an overstuffed chair. "How'd you know I was here?"

"Mama, I made an educated guess. You're parked—somehow—diagonally across the driveway. And your headlights are still on."

"Vee, it's good to see you, and Elle, thanks again for the assist," Sophie added. "Be back in a minute. I'm going to check on the twins."

Lana shot Elle a questioning glance and pointed at their mother. Elle replied with a second shrug.

"Mama, purse on the top shelf. Is everything OK? Are we still on for the games tomorrow?" Lana asked.

"Of course, dear," her mother replied. She stood and slid her bag well out of reach of little hands. "I've been looking forward to this weekend all month. And Ellie, is Dan going to be there?"

"You know he is. It's not a sanctioned event, but they want to get on everyone's dance card for next year. Still, no way he's going to miss a chance to throw. He and Paige should be around early. Why ask? You could have just called Paige on the sly."

Lana lifted Angus from his slumber and took a seat next to her sister. "Mama, Dan being there is not a big deal. Ellie's been getting along fine with him, better than me and any of my exes."

Elle held up a hand. "Since everything with Stuart and the MacUspaigs, I've been working hard to come clean and get my life back on track. I'm really trying to let all the negativity go, and that includes everything between Dan and me. I'm ready for a new start. So, Mama, you don't have to worry about Dan."

"Well, I *am* worried about Daniel. I wanted to be the first to tell you."

"Tell us what, Mama?" Lana asked with a focused stare.

"Brenda Gielles is on one of my crews in Wilmington. Her sister's best friend works for Judge Howard..." Vee paused for a moment and twisted the gold ring on her finger. She stopped and looked Elle square in the eye. "Duncan Scott was released from prison this evening."

2

Put some whisky in my coffee because it's Scotland somewhere.

— Scottish Saying

A chill breeze ran through the participants scattered across Stirling Park. Men secured their kilts and women pulled their tartan wraps a bit tighter as they waited for the warm morning sun. From behind a line of trees that split the park, a pair of speakers hummed with the Skye Boat Song played by a regiment of bagpipes. The music was punctuated by the occasional thud of a caber or heavy hammer as the athletes warmed up for the exhibition.

On the far side of the field, a makeshift village of white tents had sprung up overnight, each festooned with tartan drapes, filled coolers, and clusters of lawn chairs. Dozens of locals scurried to greet neighbors and secure a field-side spot before the competition began.

Elle and Lana stood clutching covered Styrofoam cups and contemplating a pair of food trucks parked just beyond the tent village. Elle considered each truck's menu board in turn while her sister took a tentative first sip of her coffee. Lana gave it a quick sniff and shook her head.

"Hell, baby girl, how much Irish is in this Irish coffee? You know this is a dry state park."

"Like that has ever stopped anyone," Elle replied. "A Scottish event without whisky? Not going to happen. Every single clan tent here has bottles hidden somewhere, just for honored guests, of course."

"Of course. Still, go easy on the pour next time. It's 8 a.m. and I'm getting pickled just smelling this stuff."

Despite her older sister's protests, Elle knew Lana could drink her under the table. She rolled her eyes and turned her attention back to the menu boards. "Let's get some food in you. That'll sober you up fast. So, for breakfast you can have either a Scotch egg or let's see, a Scotch egg."

"You choose."

"Well then, Scotch egg it is. So, do want them from Tart'n Tasty or Lass Call?"

Lana took a moment to think as she poured out a good portion of her coffee. "Hmmmm.... let's keep it fair and do Tart'n Tasty now. At lunch, Lass Call for shepherd's pie."

"You know the pies aren't made with real shepherd."

Lana laughed and took a long drink from her cup. "Every year the same joke, baby girl. That never gets old."

From their seat atop the still half-empty bleachers that skirted the field, the sisters unwrapped their breakfast and watched a stream of familiar faces flooding in from the main gates. Scotch eggs were one of the few family delicacies that Elle had mastered. The secret, she found, was to keep the sausage coating dry but firm by adding the right amount of mince to the mix. Finish it with a crunchy crumb shell and a dash of malt vinegar, and Elle was in heaven. Still, she had to admit to herself, Tart'n Tasty made a damn good Scotch egg.

"So, you think this will stick?" Lana asked between bites.

"You mean this athletics demo? I hope so," Elle replied. "I think it's clear the Roan Island Games aren't coming back. Even with Stuart gone, I don't expect Megan or Caroline to start them up again."

"You know, Ellie, this may be a chance for something better. Move them off Roan Island, keep them closer to St. Andrews, and bring the whole community in. This could put our little town back on the map."

"You sound like a proud member of the local chamber." Elle shook her head. Her eyes squinted as she gave her sister a suspicious smile. "Wait, what do you know?"

Lana, Elle felt, always gave up her secrets too easily. "Well, Red MacFarlane isn't so ready to give up on the Roan Games, with or without the MacUspaigs' blessings. He's putting together a board of directors and asked me to offer legal assistance."

Elle laughed. "And they didn't ask me? I'm shocked. Crushed, really."

Lana gave her little sister a wink. "Baby girl, you're single again, you've got your new job, you're out of jail.... everything's coming up Elle."

"Stop, you'll make me blush," Elle groaned. "Turning over a new leaf is hard work. They're heavier than they look." If anyone knew the challenges she had overcome, Elle knew it was her older sister. Since they were children, Lana had been her rock, the one who believed in Elle when she worried no one else would. Every time she looked in Lana's eyes, she saw nothing but pride and love reflected within.

"You know, you really knocked Mama over last night," Lana said around a mouthful of breakfast. "She hasn't shut up all morning about how you shouldn't be wasting your life doing research projects. Ten minutes into one of your murder shows, and you're already rounding up the bad guys. She swears she's going to ask Sheriff Hopkirk about making you an honorary deputy."

"It's not that hard. Just pay attention, suspect everyone, and keep an open mind. Plus, I've seen that episode like three times before." Elle snickered as Lana coughed up bits of sausage and boiled egg.

"I love you, but you are just the worst, and I say that with—" A chime from her purse cut Lana's thought short. "One sec." Pulling her cell phone from an inside purse pocket, Lana read for a few moments before dashing off a quick response. After a few more exchanges, she dropped the phone into her bag and shook her head.

"Bad news?"

"Not so much bad as it is concerning. That's Trey Howard. He's close to one of the original prosecutors on Duncan Scott's case, and he owes me a favor for some land contracts I did for him. I texted him last night to figure out why the hell they released Duncan."

"And?"

"OK, he says the details are thin, and this was done without him being in the loop. It seems that Scott's defense attorney may have submitted his plea deal without his client's knowledge or approval."

"And that's a bad thing because?"

"Ellie, you can't plea to something without meaning to. Sounds like his attorney thought it was the best he could do, so he went for it, with or without Duncan. Problem is that Duncan is what some of us would call low functioning. Nice enough guy—outside of the murder, of course—but just happy to go with the flow whether he's got a full grasp of the situation or not. There's some question as to what he did and didn't agree to vis-à-vis the plea."

"Wouldn't he have to attest to that in front of a judge?"

Lana brushed the last few crumbs off her tartan skirt, tucking the wadded paper wrapper into her bag. Elle didn't see her sister look at a loss for words often, and this time she was sure she was stalling for just a few seconds.

"That's the tricky part," Lana continued, pausing a moment to run her fingers through her hair. "This was in front of Judge Stanton. He had been on the bench for fifty years, probably more. There's no record of the pre-trial. It may have been one of those things that everyone just wanted to go away."

"OK, so there's a question. Now, my question is why is he out?"

"No idea. Trey says this whole thing has been quieter than a church mouse. After the stink the first time around, I guess they were hoping to keep it under the radar until it got sorted out. My lawyerly but not criminal-lawyerly guess is that a new judge may have vacated his plea. Duncan could have been released pending a new trial or whatever other solution they can come up with. Whatever it is, he's staying at his grandparents' farm just north of town. This is gonna get ugly."

Elle closed her eyes and inhaled. Dark concerns tumbled across the edge of her thoughts like storm clouds on a distant horizon. For the first time in the past few months, Elle was truly worried.

"Thinking about talking to Dan?" Lana asked.

Without opening her eyes, Elle nodded. She held her breath for a moment then let out a slow, steady exhale. "I want to head over and say hello before the competition starts. He's going to have trouble with his concentration as it is."

Lana turned in her seat to look her in the eye. "You don't talk much about him, but Sophie and I always figure that no news is good news." Despite the intrusion, Elle felt a sense of calm and relief having this time with her sister. Elle always respected how Lana could ask difficult questions without overreaching.

"If you step back and look at the big picture, Dan has always been a good guy. He's a great father to Paige, and his heart's in the right place."

"So, it's just another part he couldn't keep in the right place?" Lana asked. She gave Elle a gentle elbow in the ribs to underscore her blue humor. Elle couldn't help but laugh.

"Well, the official narrative is that he cheated, but down inside, I know it's more that he cheated *first*. Lana, he probably just beat me to the punch. We should never have gotten married. Should have stayed friends. It wasn't a good match back then, and I think it was obvious to everyone but us. Mostly, it was obvious to Mama."

"Everything is obvious to Mama, and she'll be the first to tell you. Honestly, I always thought you two had a chance," Lana said with a warm smile. "Baby girl, you can do anything you put your mind to."

"Anything?"

"Yes, including pushing the other woman's car into a ditch with her and Dan in the back seat. I will never, ever bet against you when you set your mind to it."

"You've really got this big sister thing down."

"Beautiful morning, ladies."

As Elle and Lana paused their walk toward the athlete's prep area, an older man in a kilt of muted salmons, blues, and greens approached them from behind and gave a vigorous wave and hearty smile. His scraggly white hair was tucked under a tam cap in a matching tartan, and in one hand, he navigated with a heavy mahogany cane.

"I was up in the booth waiting to announce the hammer toss. Now, my eyes can't read the page in front of me, but I can spot a bonnie lass at fifty paces. I looked up and saw the most lovely pair of young ladies enjoying breakfast across the field. I climbed down, but on these old legs, I was outrun, so I thought I'd stop and chat with the Cunningham girls instead." His sentence ended with a broad wink and a hearty guffaw at his own joke.

"Grady Foster, you old charmer," Lana replied with a shake of her head.

He planted his cane firmly in the freshly mown grass and gave Lana a second wink. "I was hoping to see you all this morning. Your mother here?"

Elle nodded. "She and Sophie have the twins back at our tent. She gave us five minutes for breakfast, so we took thirty."

The older man furrowed his brow and gave Elle a sincere, fatherly squint as he stroked his beard. "Spoken to Dan yet?"

Elle raised both hands in surrender. She knew she should be used to the grim efficiency of the island's gossip vines, but it still caught her off guard. "Bad news travels fast around here. And no, I haven't talked to him. We're heading over to catch him before he competes."

"I haven't heard the whole story from last night, but I've heard enough. After what happened to Daniel's mother, my poor Shona... let it suffice to say that Duncan will need to watch his step around St. Andrews. And he'd best steer clear of everyone here today if he has any sense. Sadly, I don't think he's ever been long on sense." Grady took a slow breath and gave a deep, rumbling hum.

"We will, Grady," Elle replied. As much as she admired the older man, this was a conversation she was going to soon tire of having with others. "You better be getting back."

"Ah, the hammer toss doesn't kick off for another twenty minutes, so I still have time to see if the beer tent is open this fine morn," he replied with a slight hop in his step.

Lana cast him a sideways glance. "A little early for beer and climbing up and down that tower, isn't it?" she asked.

"True, true," he replied, "but not too early to do a little courting. Off to say hello to Miss Peg and Miss Effie. Keep this old heart beating another day. Please give Dan my best." With a tip of his woolen cap, he wished the sisters a good day and turned at a spry clip toward the sprawling beer tent.

The periphery of the main field was peppered with burlap-wrapped bales of hay, pitchforks, throwing hammers, and the other staples of a Scottish competition. A few dozen women and men milled about the confines, stretching, inspecting their gear, and catching up with old friends. Their lively chatter coupled with the chill air gave the gathering an atmosphere of electricity and excitement.

Across the field, a beefy fellow in a kilt and athletic shirt crouched ahead of a caber toss. In his cupped hands, he vertically balanced a hundred-pound beam. At sixteen feet long, the practice caber measured on the short side for a competition toss but perfect for a warm-up. He brought himself to a stand, ran forward five or six paces, and gave the caber a mighty heave. It nearly flipped end over end, the top planting firmly in the grass ahead of the man. It balanced and teetered for just a second before falling back in his direction. As another athlete offered advice, the spectators gave encouraging applause.

A tall man with fading red hair hailed the sisters from a chair beneath Grady's tower. He wore a coat and kilt both in MacFarlane Modern Red. The pattern's red-and-black cross-hatching in many ways mirrored the colors of the Modern Cunningham tartan, although the stripes were of different widths and combinations.

"Lana Cunningham, so glad you could come out this morning." Red MacFarlane beamed. "And Elle, it's good to see you looking well. We haven't had a chance to talk since everything on Roan Island. Anne told me to send you her best if I saw you."

"No sense looking back," Elle replied. This was another conversation she had tired of: a once in a lifetime opportunity that had ended in tragedy. Still, she realized it was now part of their shared past, so no escaping the topic. "I'm excited that you both are looking to reboot the games."

"It's nothing quite that formal, at least not yet. We thought an impromptu exhibition for the athletes would be a nice way to test the waters. No one earns any points, but it's a chance to get on the NASGA's radar."

"Fingers crossed," Lana added. "If this dry run goes well, we can build a volunteer team, offer more on the cultural side, and include competitions for the pipers and dancers. In another year or two, we can formally launch as the St. Andrews Highland Games."

"You both know how much the games on Roan meant to Anne and me," he continued. "We were heartbroken when they were scrubbed. I've been attending since I was in high school some forty years ago."

He paused to look around at the growing crowds in their tartans and plaids. "Chances to celebrate our culture are few and far between. None of us can afford to let this one go. We are staking a great deal on the opportunity to keep Scottish heritage alive here in St. Andrews. In fact, Anne and I decided to fund most of today's events. We want this to succeed and thrive."

"Anything you need, just let us know," Lana said, taking the man's hand in hers. "Mama would never forgive us if we didn't."

"You're already doing your part, Lana, and Elle, history will be the foundation of these new games. Families like yours are the lifeblood of our community."

Another round of applause rose from the far side of the field, and Red clapped and whistled in response. The sisters bid him goodbye and skirted the stacks of gear as they approached the athletes in their preparations.

To one side of the congregation, a teen girl with dark hair and gangly limbs sat atop a pair of burlap-wrapped hay bales. Her distressed rock tee showcased a band Elle had never heard of. The shirt complemented torn jeans and scuffed high-tops, giving the girl a carefully cultivated air of simply not caring what other people thought. As the sisters approached, she looked up from her phone, smiled, and waved them over.

"Hey, Aunt Elle," the girl said as she rose to greet her with an enthusiastic hug.

"So, *Aunt Elle* is what you settled on?" Lana asked.

"We tried a couple of different things," Elle replied. "It doesn't roll off the tongue, but it sounds better than Ex-Stepmother Elle or the Woman Formerly Known as Stepmother

Elle." She turned back to the girl with a concerned look. "So, Paige, how are you doing?"

She scrunched her face and thought for a moment. "I'm OK, I guess. Just worried about Dad."

"How's he doing this morning?"

"He's OK—at least, I guess he's OK. Like as much OK as he's willing to let on." She shrugged one shoulder. "He's better now that we're here. He's totally focused on the competition, even if it's not a *real* games. I get that that's good to take his mind off everything."

For Paige's age, she was perceptive, Elle felt. She had a keen sense of empathy that her ex-stepmother found admirable. Elle gave her a second hug. "I was thinking about him last night and wanted to check in. If you see him before the sheaf toss, tell him I said hello and good luck."

"Nice try." Paige grinned and looked over Elle's shoulder. "Tell him yourself."

Elle turned to find herself nose to nose with a familiar face. Only an inch or two taller, Dan Mackay had a solid bearing that belied his height. Short, dark brown hair and a closely cropped beard obscured his age, while green eyes and a generous smile tempered his rougher features. Despite his athletic bulk, Elle found him to be disarmingly quiet when he moved.

"Holy Hell, Dan," she exclaimed under her breath. "Don't sneak up on me like that." If she were honest with herself, Elle would have admitted that she really didn't mind him sneaking up on her. She found his sudden presence a bit disorienting, but in a way she found magnetic.

"Sorry, Elle," he offered as he spread his arms to give her a quick hug. "I'm always jittery before a toss, and this morning, I'm in a weird place. I don't know where my head is. I'm hoping for the best but preparing for the worst." He looked to the other Cunningham sister with a warm smile. "Hey, Lana."

She nodded and leaned in to give him a quick peck on the cheek.

"I get it," Elle replied. "I just wanted to check in on you, so let's talk when you're done. And good luck out there today."

"Thanks, Ellie."

"And Paige, if you need anything today, swing by the tent. Mama will be there all day with soft drinks and snacks. She'd love to see you."

The girl smiled and waved them off. In the bleachers, the growing crowd began to clap and cheer as the next round of athletes took to the field.

3

It matters not how a man dies, but how he lives. The act of dying is not of importance, it lasts so short a time.

— James Boswell

At the beer tent, Effie McLeane marshaled a group of four volunteers to stack kegs behind the service tables. The short, stout woman kept her team moving with sharp direction and clear instructions. She counted and recounted the keg pyramids, making detailed notes on a worn McLeane Spirits clipboard. She wore a black, collared work shirt and dark denim jeans covered by a brilliant white apron, a combination that suggested dedicated professionalism. A few loose gray locks had escaped the snug bun on the back of her head, the only clue that perhaps the beer tent setup wasn't quite on schedule.

"This is a first-time event, everyone," she called out to the group. "No idea what we'll need on hand. We've got fourteen more kegs to make space for before alcohol tickets go on sale.

"*Fourteen*," she stressed with careful diction. Her emphasis gave the R a hard sound, somewhere between an Irish brogue and a Scottish burr.

As Elle and Lana approached, a slim woman with bright, ice-blue eyes and a short, faded brown bob struggled to straighten a McLeane tartan cloth over a plastic folding table. As her thin fingers tugged one side of the tartan sheet, the other would slip, revealing the stained surface beneath.

"Peggy, let me help you with that," Lana offered. Reaching across the table, she squared the cloth and weighted it down with a partially filled cashbox and roll of printed tickets.

"Bless you, Lana," Peg Kinnear replied. Despite her flustered composure, her movements were sharp and brisk. "I'm not myself today. Of course, you've heard about Duncan."

"Everyone has heard," Effie said from beyond the table as both sisters nodded in unison. "Orna Gunn and the rest of town's gossips have seen to that."

Peg shook her head and looked off into the distance. "I haven't seen him since that horrible afternoon, except in the papers, I guess. I'm worried sick he's going to turn up today and cause a scene. None of us are safe."

Returning to her post at the kegs, Effie clucked her tongue. "Peg, if you don't want to be here, you shouldn't have volunteered. You can leave if you need to. We can pull Orna from the gate. If you're going to stick it out, then get ready because sales open at 9:30 a.m. sharp. And not a moment earlier, no matter what Grady Foster says."

On cue, the first thirsty guests formed a line at the table, ready to exchange cash for a few drink tickets. As the queue grew, Elle caught sight of Dan joining the crowd, and she waved him up. He reluctantly obliged.

"I thought you were ready to toss?" she asked.

"Trouble with the high bar. They are doing some demonstration throws until they get it squared away. I've got twenty minutes or so. Figured I'd get tickets now before the line stretches back to the food—" He froze mid-thought, and his eyes narrowed with a flash of fury.

"Dan?" Concerned, Elle followed his sight line. Coming down the hill from the north gate, Duncan Scott made his way past the last of the clustered white tents. Undeterred by the crowds, he made a direct approach to the group at the ticket table. His clothing was worn and unwashed, and in his hand, Elle saw a small square of paper covered in faded colors.

As Peg Kinnear gave an audible gasp, Elle looked back to her ex-husband. His eyes were suddenly empty, and his body was tense. His neck began to flush deep red as his breathing faded to a shallow rasp. Elle felt her heart pound in her chest. Dan had taken two steps toward Duncan before she rushed in to grab his arm and pull him back. Lana stepped in and blocked him from any further approach.

"Dan? Listen to me. It's not worth it," she stated with a forced calm in her voice. "*He's* not worth it. You can't change anything."

As Duncan approached the table, he barely glanced in Dan's direction, nearly sidestepping the athlete's interception course.

"Do you think you can just ignore me?" Dan demanded. With one solid arm, he caught the lanky youth square in the chest, knocking him to the ground. Before Elle could intervene, Dan took a knee beside his target and grabbed the man's worn T-shirt with both fists. "What the hell are you doing here?"

He lifted Duncan's torso off the ground, bringing them nearly face to face before slamming him back to the earth. The younger man's head bounced off the packed dirt, and he let out a deep exhale. He attempted to pull himself back, but Dan held him firm.

"That's enough!" an authoritative voice commanded. A stout mahogany walking stick materialized between the two men, forcing Dan back to his knee. After a moment of contemplation, he released his grip on the tattered shirt. Duncan began to cough and wheeze as his breath returned.

"Dan." Grady Foster commanded the athlete's full attention. "You're better than this. We both held a great deal of love for your mother and would have done anything for her, but this isn't going to bring her back. Don't make this any worse than it already is."

Dan exhaled, and his shoulders fell as Elle felt she saw the crest of his rage pass. Grady offered him a hand, bringing him unsteadily to his feet. The older man gave him a hug with one arm while keeping the tip of his walking stick centered on Duncan's prone chest.

Without a word, Dan looked to Grady, then Elle, then Duncan. He spat, nearly hitting the youth's face, and stalked off toward the athletics field.

"As for you," Grady said, still pinning Duncan to the dirt path, "you know you have no business here."

"That's for me to say," he replied, pushing the stick from his chest. He stood and looked around the crowd, not finding a sympathetic face. "I'm a free man, judge said so."

"That's true, for now." The older man shook his head and pointed the cane toward the north entrance. As Elle felt her pulse slow slightly, she was grateful for the older man's authoritative presence. "Best for all involved if you head back home, Duncan. You'll find no other friends here and plenty who would wish you harm. You beat the odds once, but you shouldn't push your luck, lad."

The young man stood stiffly, casting dark glances at Grady, then Elle, Lana, and the other women around the ticket sales table. He swiped the dirt from the back of his head with one hand and tucked the colored paper into his shirt pocket with the other. He took a deep breath and visibly unclenched his jaw, waiting a long moment as though savoring it.

"Fair enough," he replied. "What I've got can wait a little longer."

"Anything you have to say is best saved for another time." Grady's walking stick emphasized the north entrance again. As though directed by Moses, the silent crowd parted, leaving Duncan a clear path back up the hill. As he passed, someone muttered "bastard" just barely under their breath.

"That's enough excitement for one morning," Grady commented to no one in particular. He looked around at the shocked faces and waved them away with his cane. "I have games to announce, and I'm sure each of you has gossip to spread. Elle, Lana, ladies." He tipped his tam to the foursome and followed Dan's path back to the main field.

After lunch, the sisters secured a spot next to the southeast corner of the field for the second half of the women's competitions. A broad-shouldered athlete, her hair dyed a vivid Kelly green, planted her feet firmly behind the wooden toe board. With both hands, she held a long rod tipped with a heavy metal ball. Elle welcomed the distraction. Cheering for someone else's Herculean efforts made her forget about the earlier scene.

As the athlete positioned herself, the small crowd began to call and whistle in a show of support. Her back to the open field, she gave the rod a series of mighty overhead swings. She released the hammer on the fourth rotation, the weight carrying it far into the grassy meadow. As it landed with a solid thump, the small crowd broke into applause as the officials marked and measured her distance.

"You go, Sheila!" Lana exclaimed with a wolf whistle. To Elle, she confided, "She keeps this up, and she'll be breaking records by the time she hits twenty." She gave her sister a curious look. "You are a million miles away, baby girl. What's going on in your head?"

"What the hell was he thinking?" she replied with a shake of her head.

"Which one? Dan or Duncan?"

"Well, I don't know…Either. Both. Duncan had no business coming here. All he could do is stir up more trouble, and Dan would have been happy to give him that trouble, justified or not."

"Everyone's been talking about this all day. Some things just don't make sense. Duncan had a bee in his bonnet, and Dan couldn't help himself. Not sure I could blame him. If something like that happened to Mama, you know we would take turns beating the living breath out of whoever did it."

"It's *whomever*, dear," Elle corrected in a poor imitation of her mother's voice. "I'm sure she'd find it comforting to know she can count on her girls to avenge her untimely demise." Elle shot a quick glance in her sister's direction, and Lana rolled her eyes.

Overhead, the afternoon sun had begun to dip toward the west. Elle rose from her lawn chair and changed the subject. "Well, amateurs will finish at 4 p.m., and it's about time to get packed up. It'll be a crush of cars loading out the tents. I don't want to wait until the last moment."

A folded chair under each arm, Lana followed her sister across the park to the shrinking village of white pop-ups.

Several families had already begun packing up in advance of the day's end. As they approached the Cunningham tent, Paige intercepted their course from the far side of the field.

"Dad wants to know if I can get a ride home," the girl called as she approached the pair.

"Is that Paige?" Vee's voice came from the tent up ahead.

"Paige and the two of us, Mama," Lana replied as their mother rose to greet them.

"Where's your father?" Vee asked.

"He can't find his pitchfork or his gloves. He had them at the field but hasn't seen them since lunch. He's looking for them but can't remember where he left them. He said it might take a while, so he wanted to see if you could take me home."

"I sent Sophie and the twins home early, so I'll need a ride," Lana added. "Four should fit, even with the tent and tables." As she entered the tent, she stacked her two folding chairs and began to dismantle their temporary camp.

Elle gently caught Paige by the arm and pulled her to one side. "How's he doing?"

The young girl screwed her lips and scrunched her nose. "He's having a bad day. After the whole thing with that Duncan creep, he whiffed all three chances on his throw. He spent the rest of the day under the big tree next to the bleachers. Never even tried on the other events. He didn't want to talk to me or anyone. Just sat there by himself. I didn't talk to him again until he came looking for his fork."

"I could go give him a hand," Lana offered from inside the tent.

"Naw, I don't think he wants the help," Paige replied. "Plus, I don't want to make everyone's day any worse."

As the words left the girl's lips, a plaintive, high-pitched scream echoed across the park. After a moment of silence, it was followed by several more desperate wails. Elle froze in place, her ears trying to estimate the source of the cries.

Lana leapt to her feet and pulled Paige into the tent. "Mama, you keep Paige here, understood?"

The girl and older woman both nodded in silence.

"Where do think it came from?" she asked Elle.

"Maybe north of here, not much else up there." Before she could finish, her older sister was already sprinting toward the north gate. As much as she admired Lana's spirit, Elle was just beginning to learn the benefits of looking before leaping. She called out and began to run after her. "What the hell are we going to do?"

"I don't know," Lana yelled as she darted down the north gate pass. "We'll figure it out when we get there."

Just past the north gate to Stirling Park lay a tranquil field of broad oak trees and seasonal clover. Though some called the area Quaker's Farm, the place had no official name. Locals, however, knew it to be a quiet spot to walk the dozen or so sun-dappled paths that crisscrossed the rural acreage. This late afternoon, the peace of the field was broken by the screams of two girls.

Lana and Elle approached from the south and found the north gate locked and unattended, as was the norm. Footpaths on either side of the roadway offered easy access into and out of the park. Following the keening wails, they found a pair of teen girls hiding behind a large oak only a few dozen feet into the field.

Lana reached the teens first and knelt beside them. "Are you both OK?"

The two nodded without speaking. One girl lifted an arm and pointed timidly at the stone wall just through the trees.

As Elle caught up with her sister, a group of three young men came around the gate. Lana waved them over. "Stay here with these two, make sure they are all right. We will be right back. Understood?"

The tall youth at the front of the pack nodded.

"What?" Elle asked. "Why are we going? Those guys look young, healthy, and willing to take any unnecessary risks."

Without an answer, Lana slipped through the trees and approached the low stone wall. Elle joined her as they stopped a few yards from a wide gap in the stonework. They both listened in silence. Aside from the hubbub of the group behind them, bird songs were the only sounds across the fields. Together, they approached the pass, watchful for any movement.

Elle gasped, her eyes locked onto the grisly scene before her. Next to the gap, a tall, weathered oak gate with rusted hinges lay leaning against the wall. Tiny flecks of sunlight filtered through the tree canopy, bathing the scene in a patchwork of lights and darks. While his body stood propped against the gate, Duncan Scott's head was pitched forward, and his motionless arms hung to each side. To Elle, he gave the impression of a grotesque marionette hanging in some forgotten corner of a puppeteer's workshop.

The only thing keeping his body from slumping to the ground was the competition pitchfork. The fork's tines had been forced through the young man's chest and downward into his abdomen. The other end of the weapon's long handle lodged into the dirt before him, pinning him against the gate like the third leg of an easel.

Elle found her biggest surprise to be the near total lack of blood. The neat, precise holes in the man's shirt had small traces of red, and a thin trail of blood had snaked down the underside of the pitchfork's handle. Where the wood shaft touched the ground, a tiny pool had begun to form in the dried leaves. Other than the presence of the deadly weapon, the scene was surprisingly free of gore or violence. Remove the pitchfork, she thought, and Duncan could have been sleeping while standing against the gate.

Elle approached the body with caution, placing each step with care to avoid anything that may later be considered important. She stood motionless for just a moment, reminding herself it wasn't the first dead body she had seen. Hell, she thought, it wasn't the first dead body I've seen this year. Still, she worried that this might be something she had grown too comfortable with.

She knelt before Duncan's still form. She saw no evidence of breathing, and his open, lifeless eyes stared past her into the unknown. She felt his neck for a pulse but couldn't feel any beat beneath the cold skin.

"He's definitely dead," she said, standing and taking a moment to check her surroundings. A handful of half-shelled pistachios lay beneath one hand with a sprinkling of empty shells around his feet. There was no sign of a struggle, not so much as a fallen leaf out of place. The only other hint of human interference lay a dozen or so feet before the gate—an open pack of cigarettes rested near a sapling oak, its contents scattered across the dirt path.

Lana joined her sister, placing her hands on Elle's shoulders as though to give them each a sense of support. As they surveyed the scene, the voices behind them grew louder. The crowd now north of the gate was expanding.

Lana called back to the group. "Everyone stay there. Please. And someone call 911. *Now!*"

"Yeah, he's definitely gone," Elle repeated.

"Oh, hell, baby girl. I have to ask, but is that Dan's fork?"

Elle took a slow inhale and exhale. She chided herself for not noticing the gear before. She nodded. "Pretty sure it is. Damn."

4

Be happy while you're living, For you're a long time dead.

— Scottish Proverb

As the late afternoon sunlight began to fade, Detective Jonah Tanner leaned against the north gate and flipped through a tiny notebook. He was dressed for a day off, his tall frame attired in an off-the-clock pairing of cargo shorts and a gray T-shirt beneath an SAPD windbreaker. With his youthful face and short, dark hair, he looked to Elle like a college student who had gotten lost on his way to the quad.

"So, one more time. The last time you saw Scott was this morning?" The detective's rich baritone voice was the only hint that he was, in fact, an officer of the law. Elle and Lana detailed the last two hours for a third time as the young man checked his notes.

"Right at 9:30," Elle confirmed. "Tickets had just gone on sale, so maybe 9:35 after everything with Dan and Grady was done."

"And neither of you saw Dan after that?"

Elle gave the detective a withering look. "No, but I'm sure a few hundred people watched him compete and then cool off under the big oak."

"Well, I'll confirm his morning as soon as I ask them." He flipped back a few pages. "And other than that, nothing unusual or worth mentioning until you heard the girls screaming?"

"Nope. Nothing. And that was about 3:30, give or take."

"Yeah, according to the girls, they had slipped out the north gate to sneak a few cigarettes. Hopefully, the shock will put them off smoking for a few more years."

Lana shook her head. "This part was all a rush. One second, we were chatting up Paige and Mama, and the next, we hear the most awful wailing. We were just worried that someone had gotten hurt."

Elle groaned. "Someone *did* get hurt."

As she finished her thought, a booming voice called out from the path behind her.

"Tanner, I need to know that you're going to do something about this." With his call to action, Red MacFarlane had separated himself from the crowd beyond the gate and began to approach the detective. His face was ruddy, and his voice hinted at desperate agitation.

The young policeman tucked his notebook in his windbreaker pocket and raised his hands in a calming motion. "We are doing everything we can, Mr. MacFarlane," he offered in a reassuring tone. "It's only been a few hours, and we have the situation under control."

The older man huffed up, his mouth open and ready to argue, but nothing came out. After a few moments, he managed, "We have put a great deal of effort and resources into today's event. I can't say that justice wasn't done here today, but the timing was unfortunate. The sooner this is resolved, the sooner it will be forgotten."

Jonah reached into his back pocket and withdrew his wallet. From it, he extracted a worn, white business card. He offered it to the man with a look of serious concern. "I promise you, we are working as hard as we can to get closure, but it's only been a few hours. Things will look much clearer tomorrow. This is my card. If you have any questions at any time, you can call me on my personal cell phone."

Red accepted the card with a mixture of nervousness and worry. Without a word, he turned on his heel and returned to the group congregating beyond the fence.

As Elle watched him depart, she noticed a pair of men standing just outside of the crowd. Grady Foster leaned against his mahogany walking stick while his left hand rested on the shoulder of a taller man with a rough beard and long brown ponytail. He was dressed in a denim kilt with an unadorned black T-shirt. His heavy boots were better intended for hiking than Scottish sports.

It was his eyes, though, that had caught Elle's attention. Even from a distance, she could feel them bearing down on her. Despite Grady's attempts to draw the man into conversation, his unblinking gaze never left Elle, her sister, and the young detective. It gave Elle a visceral chill she couldn't shake.

Jonah followed her line of sight and gave a low whistle. "Kelsey has it in for one of us."

"I don't need a second guess," Elle added. "He's never been a fan of mine."

Three years younger than her ex-husband, Kelsey Mackay was several inches taller with a temper several degrees hotter. He and Elle had never been close, the difficulties between her and Dan often bleeding over into the brothers' relationship.

"We've had our run-ins, too. Mostly drunk and disorderlies, a pair of DUIs, and at least one restraining order I know of." Jonah pulled out his notebook and dashed off a few words. "Of course, that plus a few extra dead bodies sums up our relationship, too, Elle." She shot him a dirty look, relieved for an excuse to turn away from Kelsey's glare. "I haven't talked to him yet, but he's near the top of the list. Duncan killed his mother, and Kelsey isn't one for controlling his temper."

"True. Honestly, it was a damn good thing that Duncan found Dan earlier and not Kelsey. Kelsey would have probably killed him there and then, with or without the crowd. Speaking of Dan, are you really going to take him in?"

"Jeannie has already driven him down to the station," he replied. "He went willingly, I should add. And he's not under arrest. We are just asking him some questions. Kelsey will be getting the same treatment, even if we aren't expecting the same cooperation." Despite his assurances, Elle's eyes turned cold, giving the detective an unfriendly stare.

"Elle, look at this from the outside. Duncan killed their mother, but it was Dan that threatened Duncan earlier today. Dan's fork is kind of key to this whole thing, and Dan can't account for his entire time at the competition. Listen, I've known Dan probably longer than you have. I get it. But on this one, it's best that I just go by the book."

Lana wrapped one arm around her sister's shoulders. "Ellie, this is going to work out. Just let Jonah do his job."

Elle shrugged, she hoped conveying how unconvinced she was. "I don't know if Dan has his phone with him," she added, "but he isn't answering. Please let him know that we are taking Paige home. She can stay with us until he's ready to pick her up."

OFF SCOT FREE

―――――――――――――――

Sophie Cunningham-Klein ended a call, slipped her phone into a robe pocket, and curled up in an easy chair across from the den sofa. The sleeping basset hound took the lion's share of the couch, while Elle made do with the few remaining inches of comfort.

"Lana is dropping your mom off at home, and she'll swing by Ollie's Liquor for some Irish Cream," Sophie said. "Our bottle keeps disappearing."

"Hmmm... curious," Elle replied with mock surprise.

"I can call her back if you want anything else. I'm not much of a drinker, but today has me hankering for a smoky bourbon."

"I appreciate it, but I'm fine. I've been trying to downshift my social drinking game, but Irish Cream is the one vice I can't entirely kick." She knew her sister-in-law was well versed on the number and variety of Elle's vices, but she appreciated the woman's easygoing concern.

"Well, it's been a hell of a day. So, you've earned a little vice if you need it."

"How's Paige?" Elle asked, trying to change the subject.

Sophie bobbed her head a bit. "I think she's OK. She's up with the twins, reading them a bedtime story. Lana made a few calls, and Dan should be home either later tonight or in the morning. He's still not under arrest, but they are going over everything for the hundredth time. Either way, it's best that Paige crashes here until he's home."

The pair sat in silence for a few minutes. Deep in sleep, Angus occasionally broke the welcome quiet with a gentle snore.

"Elle, if this is off limits, let me know," Sophie began, "but what happened to Dan's mother? It isn't something Lana and I talk about. We met about the same time you and Dan started dating, and I guess Shona had already died by then. I read a few things in the papers, but I was finishing up school at that point, so it already felt like distant history by the time I came back to St. Andrews."

"No, that's not off limits," Elle replied. She shifted in her seat as she thought of the right words. "Honestly, it wasn't something Dan and I discussed much either. If anything, I think he and I were a way for him to avoid everything surrounding her murder. I was a rebound, and I don't think I minded much. We were both running away from things we didn't want to deal with."

"Can you give me the short, sanitized version?" Like her wife, Sophie had mastered the art of asking intimate questions without crossing boundaries. Elle knew that she herself hadn't yet developed that particular skill.

"It's sad, but there's not much to the whole thing. Dan's mother, Seonag—everyone called her Shona—lived over off Selkirk on the north end of St. Andrews. And this was all before Dan and I were even dating.

"She did bookkeeping for some of the local businesses. Seemed well-liked by everyone. Dan worshipped her." She shrugged and shook her head. "Nothing really out of the ordinary about her."

"Where did Duncan come in to all this?"

"Duncan was just one of our St. Andrews locals. Nice enough guy, but always a little off. You know, that one neighbor or cousin everyone says is perfectly fine for company but just not quite right. And not in a bad way, just got an elevator that doesn't always go to the top floor."

Sophie gave an encouraging laugh. "Yup, in my family that's my cousin Sheila."

"Yeah, I'm beginning to worry that in the Cunningham clan, I'm that cousin," Elle confessed with a smile. She had discovered over the past few years that conversations with her sister-in-law left her feeling relaxed and heard.

"Elle, they all adore you," Sophie said, grinning from ear to ear. "You keep things interesting. And between the slow and steady of Lana and your mama, a little extra interesting is a good thing."

"Sophie, you're an angel. Consider me comforted. Now, back to Duncan. He lived a bit north of town, just past the field where they found him. His grandparents have a farm, for lack of a better word because I have no idea if they actually farm anything, up there. Duncan had always been pretty good with trade skills, so he'd do light handyman work or whatever for the housewives around St. Andrews."

Sophie leaned back in her chair and nodded slowly. "I think every town has a few Duncans around."

"So, about six or seven years ago, just before the end of summer break, Duncan had been working at Shona's house and a few others in the neighborhood. In the middle of the day, he just walked off. Disappeared. Maybe an hour later, a neighbor found Shona's sliding glass backdoor ajar and Shona dead inside."

"Oh, God," Sophie gasped. "That's horrible." Angus lifted his head at the noise and looked around the room. Failing to sense an intruder, he let his head fall back to the sofa cushion, his ears folding over Elle's leg. She gave them a quick scratch, taking a moment to get the fine details correct.

"She had been strangled, and some jewelry had been taken. A few hours later, they caught Duncan hiding on his grandparents' farm. He denied any involvement, but there was a stack of evidence against him. Based on all that, Duncan pled guilty to her murder in exchange for getting the death penalty off the table."

Sophie sighed and let her eyes trail off to the windows overlooking the back deck. "That must have been hell for Dan," she said after several moments.

"I'm sure it was," Elle replied. "It may sound terrible, but we just never discussed it. He didn't bring it up, and I didn't want to ask. That was pretty much the unwritten rule of our relationship. Don't ask, don't tell. And you can see how far that got us."

Sophie pulled out her phone and dashed off a quick text.

"I'm hoping it's not too late for Lana to get that bourbon."

5

Danger and delight grow on one stalk.

— Scottish Proverb

From her morning perch opposite the tiny courthouse in St. Andrews, Elle watched Jonah Tanner exit the old brick building, finish a mobile call, then dodge a pickup truck as he crossed the street to Elle's park bench. He had only made detective a few years prior, and his boyish face lent no gravitas to his presence. He was, Elle thought, growing into the role nicely. He had an open mind, a keen eye, and a strong sense of justice that served him well.

"You promised coffee," he said as he dropped onto the bench beside her. His smile was genuine, a trait that Elle found endearing.

She lifted a cup from a brown bag. "Iced coffee. Four creams, six sugars. It'd be easier if you just had a mocha milkshake."

He took the cup and sampled the drink. He grimaced. "Still can't stand the taste, but I've sworn off sodas for Lent." He was wearing slacks, a light sports coat, and an Oxford shirt with a necktie. The knot was off-center, but he had clearly made an effort to glow up his weekend casuals.

"Court today?" she asked, looking him up and down.

"On a Sunday? My niece is getting baptized this morning, but I'm on call. I'm going to try and swing by the church before ten. It's better than nothing, but I don't like that it's keeping me away from this Scott murder."

"So, what do you have for me?"

"Nothing, really. I just needed the caffeine." He gave her a brief glimmer of a smile.

Elle saw her opening and took it. "Well, if you've got nothing, how about I give you my few cents' worth?"

"I doubt I could stop you."

"Very true," Elle replied. She and Jonah had gone toe to toe over the past several years. In the past, they were unevenly matched: he had a badge, and she usually had a hangover—or worse. Now that she was back on her game, she agreed. She doubted he could stop her, too.

He took another sip of the coffee mix, his lips curling into the same grimace. "So, what, in your expert opinion, puts your ex-husband in the clear?"

"It's a couple of things." Elle began to count on her fingers for emphasis. "First, I've watched Dan toss the sheaf dozens of times."

Jonah screwed his face then smiled. "Is that a euphemism I should know?"

"Nice try. It's the hay bale toss—with the pitchfork. He's been nationally ranked on and off for the past seven years."

"OK, so what about it?" He swirled the coffee vigorously in its cup; his expression suggested it did nothing to improve the taste.

"When Lana and I found Duncan, the pitchfork tines were pointed downward." She tried to pantomime the action with her hands. Jonah's open mouth hinted that she might be losing him. "OK, his killer held the fork parallel to the ground, with the tines angled down, like this. That's the opposite of how you'd pitch a bale. The tines went into him, then down until they got stuck in the gate."

Jonah shrugged. "So, how does that clear Dan?" He set the coffee cup on the bench, apparently giving up. Elle was encouraged to watch him pull a pen and the tiny notebook from his jacket pocket.

"It may not, but athletes always keep the tines facing up. It's a more natural lifting motion." Her hand motions seemed to be clarifying her point, at last. "Plus, if you were trying to kill someone, you'd get far more leverage this way. It would use gravity and the person's own weight against them. I sincerely doubt that Dan—or any other athlete, for that matter—would use the fork the other way. It doesn't make sense."

"Point taken," Jonah replied, adding a few words to his notebook. "But it may also have been a heat-of-the-moment thing. Maybe Dan wasn't thinking about style points."

Elle extended a second finger. "Think about that. If it was Dan, I doubt this was a sudden attack. Let's say you are Duncan, hanging out by the stone wall. You see Dan coming up from the north gate, carrying a pitchfork. Do you think you'd stop and have a nice conversation with the man who just threatened your life? Particularly when Dan was clearly angry enough to skewer you." She paused to let the questions sink in. Jonah nodded then motioned for her to continue. "It had to be someone that didn't set off alarms for Duncan. It wasn't an obvious threat, or at least it was a threat he didn't recognize."

The detective made a few more notes then tapped the pen on the paper as he considered her words. "Two good points, I'll grant you that. Neither one, though, is a slam dunk for Dan's innocence."

Elle smiled. "I'm not done yet." She continued to a third finger. "One more: why would Dan use a pitchfork to attack Duncan? It's cumbersome, unwieldy, and doesn't make for a stealthy approach. Dan and just about every other athlete has a *sgian-dubh* on them at all times. Makes for a much better hand-to-hand weapon."

Jonah stopped scribbling for a moment. "A what?"

"The *skeen doo*," Elle repeated, using the anglicized term. "The dagger most of the guys carry in their sock. It's really for eating and all, but it makes for a perfectly serviceable weapon when you need one."

Jonah narrowed his eyes and shook his head. "I don't know, Elle."

She held up the three fingers a second time to underscore her point. "Come on, Jonah, you and I have both seen the damage a short blade like that can do. Plus, it's a hell of a lot less conspicuous than a five-foot pitchfork. Dan may have been angry, but he's not stupid."

The detective closed his notebook and drummed the cover a few times with his fingers. "You've got some good ideas, creative as always. I promise I'll keep them in mind as this moves forward. For now, though, we're playing it by the book."

Elle felt her neck and shoulders relax as the anticipation of their talk was now in the past. It wasn't a homerun, she thought, but it was a solid base hit. "I appreciate it, Jonah. Dan's had a lousy couple of years, and I don't want to see him hit rock bottom. I've been there, and it's not as fun or as liberating as I had imagined."

Jonah cocked his head to one side and gave her a curious look. "I thought you two ended on pretty sour terms."

"It was a mutually agreed upon cease-fire," Elle replied. "The hard feelings have already faded a bit. He's a solid guy. If it's not Dan—and notice I'm still saying if—do you have any ideas on who else it could be?"

Jonah shook his head and tucked his notebook into his jacket pocket. "This is strictly off the record for now, but the coroner is saying he was killed before lunch. She can't give an exact time, but that's her best guess. The twist is that anyone could have followed him to the north gate. With all the milling about that morning, everyone had an opportunity."

"Plus, it looked like he had been at the wall for a while," Elle added, "if the pistachio shells are any indication."

"Yup. It was an out-of-the-way area with easy access. No one would have a problem getting to Duncan and back without being noticed, even when carrying a pitchfork. Unless forensics comes back with something we didn't see, this will be an uphill climb." Jonah smiled. "You're a good person, Elle Mackay. You've had your rough patches, but you keep climbing. First, Stuart and now, Dan; you really stick by your people. I admire that."

"You'll do your best on this, and that's considerable," Elle replied with a broad smile. Jonah didn't give compliments freely, and she couldn't help but take his words to heart. "You're a good person, too, Jonah Tanner. For a cop. And this is coming from a hardened ex-con."

"Hardened?" He laughed in spite of himself. "A few days in county for mouthing off to a judge doesn't give you the street cred you think it does."

Elle snickered then caught herself. "One more thing I had almost forgotten about. Did Duncan have a piece of paper on him, maybe three or four inches on a side? May have been a photo or a magazine cutting?"

Jonah thought for a moment and shook his head. "Not that I remember. I did a quick search of his pockets at the scene, but he didn't have anything on him but his housekeys, maybe five dollars in cash, and a pocketful of pistachios. Why?"

"I'm not 100% sure," she replied with a shrug. "He was holding something like that when he first confronted Dan. He made a point of picking it up off the ground when Grady split them up. I just thought if it was important to him and now it's missing, it might be important to you."

"I'll double-check, but I'd remember something like that. One sec, Elle." From his shirt pocket, Jonah retrieved a vibrating cell phone. After a few words, he dropped the phone back in its place. "Elle, why don't you hang out for a few minutes? Maybe grab that bench in front of headquarters next door. I have to run."

Ten minutes later, Dan Mackay stepped out the front door of Police Headquarters and shielded his eyes against the morning sun. Still dressed in his kilt and competition gear, he looked ragged and defeated. He caught sight of Elle and shook his head.

"What the hell are you doing here?" he asked without malice. He took the spot next to her on the bench and leaned back into a stretch.

"Jonah tipped me off that you might be coming out soon. How are you doing?" Despite their history, Elle couldn't help but feel concern for her ex-husband. They had both made their mistakes, but beneath it all, he was still a caring father and a potential friend.

"I'm not going to lie, Elle. I've had better nights. Also had worse, but not by much."

"Why'd they keep you all night? Jonah said you weren't under arrest."

"I wasn't, at least not officially. Between questions and waiting and more questions, we didn't finish up 'til after eleven. I fell asleep on the break room couch, and Jonah didn't want to wake me. So, he let me sleep. I woke up about an hour ago, called Paige, and clarified a few more things for them. Kelsey was here for about half an hour last night. I think he answered one or two questions and then told them to go to hell."

"You look like hell." She knew she was being kind. He looked, she thought, far worse than hell. The bags under his eyes and the pauses in his words and movements took her back to a time when they were still, for the moment, married.

"I feel like hell." He paused for a second. "So?"

"What?" She looked around, as though the answer were laying in plain sight.

"Aren't you going to ask me if I did it?"

Elle grimaced and shook her head. "Dan, I know you better than that. You are hurting, but you aren't stupid. I've never once seen you react out of anger. There's no way this was you."

He exhaled and let his shoulders relax, his head tilting forward slightly. "Thanks, Ellie. And thanks for hanging out here for me."

"Want some breakfast? I'm driving."

"No, but I will take a ride home for me and Paige."

After a few blocks of driving in silence, Elle looked over to Dan, his eyes closed and his breathing shallow. Her instinct to let him sleep fought with her need to know. The need to know won. "Do you mind if I ask what happened?" she asked gently, not sure she'd get a response.

"Hell if I know," Dan replied slowly, his eyes still closed. "I completely flubbed my three throws. I figured the best plan was to sulk and feel sorry for myself. So, I did, right under the big oak next to Grady's tower." He paused for a few moments, opened his eyes, and stretched his arms. "After a while, I was feeling more hungry than sulky, so I got a few bridies from Lass Call. Then some more sulking. I think I fell asleep for a bit in the shade. Let's see. A little more sulking, then screaming. That part I remember clearly. I panicked because I didn't know where Paige was, so I checked your tent. I was with Paige and Vee until Jonah showed up. I never even went near the north gate."

"I'm glad you stayed out of it."

He looked over at her and smiled. "And somehow, you didn't. Why is it always you that ends up in the middle of things like this? You're turning into a magnet for dead bodies."

She looked back at him and gave a sheepish shrug of her shoulders. "Just lucky, I guess," she replied as she pulled into her sister's driveway. She put the car in park and left the engine idling.

Dan gave a weak laugh. "Yeah, you marry *and* divorce someone, and you think you know them. Then, bam, the bodies start piling up."

She shook her head and held his gaze for a moment. "I think that was part of our problem, Dan. I don't think we really knew each other."

"Agreed."

"You know, in all the time we were together, you never once mentioned your mother. Not once."

Dan sighed and turned away from Elle to look out the car window. "Oh Ellie, don't take it personally. It's not a conversation I wanted to have. Not with you or with anyone." He leaned back in the seat, clasping his fingers behind his head. "One day, you're talking to your mother on the phone. She's your friend, your light, your first memory. The next day, she's gone. And for what? A couple of rings that aren't worth a hundred bucks."

He paused to take a series of deep breaths, his eyes red and glistening. A tear welled up and slipped down his cheek, which he quickly wiped away.

"I can't do this right now, Elle. There's a lot of emotion going on. I still haven't talked to Kelsey."

She rubbed the back of his neck and gave his shoulder a gentle squeeze. Despite her desire to know more, she couldn't bring herself to cause Dan even a few moments of additional pain. "The whole time I've known you, I don't think I ever saw you cry."

"Elle, I cried a lot when you left."

"Honestly, I never saw it."

6

She had the best kind of courage, or maybe the worst kind, the kind that gets you into trouble.

— Alistair MacLean

"I'm not usually in on Sundays, but I've got a lot of insurance paperwork to get caught up on," Sophie said as she pulled her car keys from the hook next to the door. The rest of the Cunninghams and Mackays were spread around the home's living room. "Dan, I can drop you both off at your truck. Stirling Park is less than five minutes from my office. I'd be happy to do it."

"We can call a car. Paige has the app." He stood and offered his daughter a hand.

"Dad, really? Sophie said it's no problem," she replied, standing but never looking up from her phone.

Lana nodded in agreement. "I've got the kids, and Sophie was heading out anyway."

He sighed. "You all are the best ex-in-laws a guy could have."

Lana gave his hand a quick squeeze. "Yeah, it looks like you two are stuck with us."

Sophie leaned over the living room chair and gave her wife a kiss on the cheek. "The twins are sleeping. I should be home by five, six at the latest. Dinner is dealer's choice."

As Elle stood, Dan gave her an exhausted hug. "Thanks again, Elle. I owe you one."

"Anytime, Dan. No more keeping score, though."

As the front door closed behind the trio, Elle took the overstuffed chair next to her sister. She lay back and covered her eyes as the pair sat in silence.

After a few minutes, Lana spoke. "How's he doing?"

"OK. Not great, but OK."

"And he's in the clear with Jonah?"

"Not by a long shot," Elle replied. "He's obviously a suspect until they can prove otherwise or find someone else they like better."

Lana leaned over and rested her head on her younger sister's shoulder. It reminded Elle of a far easier time when things like loss and death only happened in books. "Is he in the clear with you?" Lana asked.

"Yup. I'm certain that Dan had nothing to do with this."

"Baby girl, I don't want to be a wet blanket, but it was Dan's fork sticking Duncan to that gate."

"I know, and that's the problem. If it wasn't Dan—and it wasn't—then why did someone pick Dan's gear? There were maybe fourteen or fifteen men and women in the sheaf toss. Why not use one of their forks?"

Lana used her toes to kick off her walking shoes. She sat up straight and flexed her toes. "Convenience? Coincidence? Could be a hundred different reasons."

Elle shook her head. "I don't buy it. Dan's mother is killed, her killer is released then killed, and Dan's fork is the weapon of choice. There must be something else going on here."

Lana sighed. "And you are the one who's going to find out what it is?"

"Of course."

"What the devil are you doing here? Where are my grandbabies?"

Elle looked up from her spot stretched out on the couch, her feet propped up on the side table. "Mama, keep it down. The twins are napping. Me too, or at least I was..."

Vee dropped her purse on the den sofa. Beside it, she deposited a toy store bag filled with stuffed animals and jigsaw puzzles. After a withering look from Elle, she reconsidered and moved the purse to a top shelf.

Although her red hair had long faded to a warm silver, Vee Cunningham moved with the surety and quickness of a woman half her age. A well-respected business owner among St. Andrews' elite, Elle always imagined Vee as an early prototype of the modern woman, balancing work, family, and a healthy social schedule. She envied her mother's passion for life, one that only seemed to evolve and deepen as she entered her seventies.

"Where's everyone else? And why aren't you at work?" With a free hand, she tried to move her daughter's feet from the furniture. Elle found that passive resistance worked best in situations like this. The dead weight of her legs never budged.

Distracted by her mother's questions, Elle found the remote under her neck pillow and put the television on pause. "Sophie is at the office, and Lana went to the ValleyMart. As for me, it's Sunday, Mama."

"How can you tell? You're here every day."

Elle sighed. "I'm working from home, Mama. Coira is in the Bahamas for three weeks, so most of us are working remotely." This was another conversation she had quickly tired of.

"So, what does working remotely even mean?" Her mother side-eyed her as her mouth twisted, like the very words themselves were suspicious.

"It means more naps and more murder TV," Elle replied, pointing the remote at the screen.

"Oh Lord, Ellie. I'd think you would have had enough murder for one weekend."

"It's much easier to deal with when it's on the TV screen."

Vee shook her head and began to straighten the magazines on the ottoman. "Which one is this?" she asked.

"That couple that disappeared off their yacht in Pamlico Sound back in the '90s."

"The Pendletons. Did you know that I knew Sarah Pendleton when she was just Sarah Carson in Wilmington?" Vee shook her head as though lost in thought. "Then she met that husband of hers, and he whisked her off to Raleigh. Two years later and they had disappeared off the face of the earth."

Elle's spirits perked up after this minor revelation. "Any idea what happened to them?"

Vee shook her head. "No idea. Kelly Delany who worked for me back then also did some cleaning for the place Sarah and her husband kept on Nags Head. She swears that the mister had more money than sense. May have gotten in over his head with the wrong kind of people. But that's just a rumor."

"And heaven forbid we should spread an unfounded rumor," Elle replied. Whether it was called gossip, neighborhood hearsay, or competitive intelligence, she knew her mother was a master at collecting whispered tidbits from all around St. Andrews.

Vee dismissed her daughter's dig with a wave of one hand. "Ellie, you know that gossip is the best way to pick up news in a town like this. You just have to know who to trust and whose word to take with a grain of salt. Still, it's gruesome to think that someone's life and death can end up as an episode of one of these trashy shows. Do you think you'll ever see Roan Island on one of these shows?"

"You know, Mama, I've gotten a couple of offers for my story. It would be easy money, but there's no way I would even consider it."

"I guess it's different when it's someone you don't know. Still, it would make one heck of a movie."

"I've already lived it once. I have no desire to see it again."

Her mother shifted gears, dropping her tone and volume to a gentler level. "I don't want to pry, Ellie, but how is Dan doing? I had heard he was with the police all night, and I was so worried about him."

"He's fine, Mama," she replied as she looked up from the TV. "And yes, you do mean to pry. You're damn good at it." Along with gossiping, prying was something her mother had mastered over the years. Elle knew how well the two went hand in hand.

"I don't know where you got your vocabulary," Vee scolded. "There are a number of rumors going around town, and I don't want to fan the flames of gossip in St. Andrews."

"*Everyone's* talking about it?"

"Honestly, yes. Half are saying that Dan gave Duncan Scott what was coming to him. Let me adjust that a bit. Nearly half are saying it was Dan with a few saying it was Kelsey. Either way, they are being made out as heroes for righting the wrongs of our crooked justice system or some such nonsense."

"And the other half?"

"The usual," her mother answered with a shrug. "There's a pitchfork-wielding maniac out to kill us all. Lock your doors and hide your children. Of course, you'd think someone like that who was committed to the idea of killing someone with a pitchfork would have thought to bring their own with them."

Elle laughed, dropping her feet to the floor in appreciation of her mother's attempt at dark humor. "Excellent point, Mama."

From the kitchen, the sound of a slamming door was followed by the rustle of paper grocery bags. Lana entered from the hall, giving her mother a kiss on the top of her head.

"Hey, Mama," she added in her smooth North Carolina drawl. "Are you staying for dinner? Sophie gave me the choice, so it's probably frozen pizza."

"Hello, sweetheart. I would love to, but I have soup in the crockpot. I'm going to run upstairs for just a second to see the sleeping angels, then I'll be out of your hair."

Vee stood and excused herself to the hall, silently making her way up the stairs. While Elle and Lana listened carefully, the creak of a door disappeared under squeals of "Grandma!" and "Granny!"

"So much for a little quiet time for me," Lana commented while putting away groceries. "What did Mama want?"

"She was hoping for the grandkids, but had to settle for me," Elle replied, joining her sister in the kitchen. As she stacked cans of vegetables and boxes of mac and cheese in the pantry, she unwrapped and pocketed a few cookies from the day's haul.

"Did she ask about Dan?"

"Not as much as I thought she would. It was more like she was just double-checking her facts. I'm thinking her network of maids, gossips, and busybodies got her most of what she needed. I was her backup. Still, she gave me an idea."

Lana paused and turned to her sister. "An idea about what, specifically?"

"Hear me out on this one," Elle began as she perched on a stool at the kitchen island. "These days, every crime has a movie or a book or a television show or a podcast or whatever. It's inevitable. Before the bodies are cold, you've got some wanna-be investigative journalist sharpening their pencils and scheduling interviews. I thought I might be able to use that to help Dan out and figure out what exactly happened to Duncan."

Lana paused her restocking of the crisper drawer. She looked to her sister, then shook her head. "Ellie, that's what the police do. If he's innocent, and we both know he is, it's their job to clear him."

"You have more faith in the system than I do." Elle's personal experience gave her a respect for Jonah and his colleagues. Her past, however, left her wary of her town's authorities. "I know they do their best, but this could be a life changer for Dan and Paige. Any help I can give, I'm going to give it."

"OK," Lana sighed as she stacked four boxes of crackers against her chest. "I'll bite. What's the big idea?"

"I'm known as a writer and researcher."

From the pantry, Lana replied, "And a smart-mouthed ex-wife with a surprisingly short fuse."

"All right, I'm primarily known as a writer and researcher. Why not research Duncan's life and death? I can talk to people, ask questions, say I'm writing a book about it."

"But to what end, Ellie?" She shook her head. "And what about Dan? Is this something he really wants you digging around? Everything you've told me says that he wants to leave this buried as deep as he can."

"By the time Dan hears about this, I'll have what I need."

"And what do you need?"

"I want to find out what happened to Duncan Scott and why someone is trying to mix Dan up with his murder. If someone is working against Dan, he's going to need me in his corner."

"I'm not a hundred percent on board with this. I want that on record," Lana replied. "Where are you going to start?"

"I'm going back to the beginning. And I need a favor. Do you have one of those official-looking, leather note pad things?"

"The word is *folio*." Lana groaned. "Fine. Let me check my office."

7

I suppose it's like the ticking crocodile, isn't it? Time is chasing after all of us.

— J. M. Barrie

Monday morning broke with a brilliant blue sky, with tiny white clouds carried across by the coastal breeze. As Elle drove north of town, she passed the entrance to Stirling Park. Streetlights and paved roads gave way to dust and scrub. Just after Highway 74, she veered off to the left just past signs pointing right to the Battleship North Carolina Museum. After another half mile, she turned down a dirt road, ignoring the No Trespassing signs that flanked the narrow drive.

Up ahead, a ramshackle farmhouse—what her mother would refer to as a folk house—sprawled beneath a pair of live oaks. The paint had long since peeled off the woodwork, and window screens sagged in their frames. On one corner of the roof, carefully spaced bricks secured a frayed blue tarp.

In the yard, piles of scrap metal choked each side of the house. A discarded washing machine and a pair of rusting box springs lay propped against a tilted cistern. Everywhere else, weeds and waist-high grass created safe havens for snakes and vermin.

At the end of an overgrown river stone walkway, a shiny red hatchback baked in the sun. Elle parked beside it and climbed the front porch steps with caution. Despite the presence of weathered window shakers, the front door was open. A patched screen door kept the bugs at bay. Elle gave the door a sharp knock and backed up a few steps.

A woman—Elle guessed her age to be about the same as her own—came to the screen door without opening it. She was above average height, black hair pulled back into a bun. She wore a white, long-sleeved blouse and khaki pants, her shoulders covered with a pale green cardigan.

"Are you with the police?" the woman asked. "If so, you missed your friends. They were here all day yesterday." Her voice gave hints of an Appalachian accent, a curious dialect born of Colonial English structures and Scottish lowland pronunciations.

"No, ma'am," Elle began.

"From the news?"

"No, just an acquaintance from St. Andrews."

"I didn't know Mrs. Scott had any acquaintances left in town. Regardless, she isn't up for sitting with guests."

"If she's sleeping, I can come back later."

The woman shook her head. "She'll never be up for guests. Since the stroke, Mrs. Scott doesn't do much but nap and watch the clouds go by."

Elle saw an opening. "I hadn't heard. I am truly sorry I hadn't stopped by before. It must have been ten years since I last saw her. I know it's no excuse, but I moved to Greenville a while back. It's too easy to lose touch. I heard what happened to Duncan, and I wanted to pay my condolences."

OFF SCOT FREE

The woman cocked her head, looking Elle up and down. "Why don't you come inside?" she offered after a few moments, unlatching the screen door. Elle followed her into the house's front room. Turned wood furniture dotted the space; a small sofa and trio of easy chairs were covered in worn quilts and crocheted throws. In one corner, an old-fashioned wood stove stood cold while a drooping ceiling fan stirred the musty air.

Near the front window, a woman with gray hair sat in a wheelchair, looking out over the North Carolina scrub. She was neatly dressed, her hands folded across the lap blanket that draped her legs. She didn't move except to breathe, but her eyes tracked the clouds that scurried across the sky.

"Angela," the woman said, offering her outstretched hand.

"Elle Cunningham. I hadn't heard about the stroke."

Angela stepped to the old woman and adjusted her blanket. She moved the wheelchair back a few inches to keep the direct sun off her charge's arm.

"Happened about two years ago, about the same time lung cancer took Mr. Scott. By the time the ambulance got all the way out here, the damage was done. Most days, I just read to her or leave her to her thoughts, whatever they may be."

"Is it just you?" Elle asked.

"No, I'm one of three. We take turns coming out each week. I spend a day or two with her, see to her needs. She'd do better in an assisted living home, but Mr. Scott was adamant she would want to stay here."

"I never realized the Scotts could afford this kind of care." Elle crossed the room as she spoke, her eyes focused on rows of pictures that hung in dollar frames between half-filled bookshelves. In many of them, Duncan Scott's face was shown through the years. He sported a school baseball uniform, held up a prize catch, took the arm of a beaming prom date, and stood beside a new bicycle.

Over the course of a dozen pictures, he grew from a child to a young man. Elle saw it as a testament to the fact that he once existed and once was loved. By the clothing styles and fading pigments, the pictures seemed to end several years ago. They simply stopped, leaving gaps on the wall to suggest a home for what might have been. Elle's heart ached for the boy who turned into a young man then simply disappeared from the wall.

"I wouldn't have imagined they could either, but the service keeps paying me to show up. Mr. Scott never discussed this sort of thing with us, but I understand that the family owned most of what you can see from the house. It really wasn't much of anything, but now that everyone's coming to St. Andrews, even the scrubland is worth something. When he knew his time was near, he made a deal with a developer out of Wilmington."

In the squares of glass covering the faded photos, Elle could see the woman watching her. She had a calm demeanor, one that suggested thoughtful attention and a pride in professionalism.

"They bought the land for I'm guessing a tidy sum," she continued. "That probably pays for her care. According to my supervisor, Mr. Scott made himself a promise that she got to stay on here until she died. Who knows when that will be, though. Could be tomorrow, could be ten years from now."

"And now that Duncan's gone?"

"We'll be sitting here until she is ready to meet her maker."

The woman stood and straightened the fabric of her khakis, adjusting the corners of her cardigan. She made her way between the simple furnishings to the open wall that held cabinets and a kitchen sink. From the dish drainer, she took out a plastic cup and turned on the tap.

"Can I offer you some water or juice? I'm afraid we don't have much else."

"No, thank you," Elle replied.

Angela gave her an inviting smile as she returned with a cup of water, and they settled into two armchairs. "So, Miss Cunningham, how long have you known Mrs. Scott? Were you one of her friends from Myrtle Beach? I know she loved spending summers with everyone down there."

Elle gave a reassuring smile. "We've been friends on and off since I was a girl. My mother and she were friends in Myrtle Beach."

Angela raised one eyebrow and shook her head.

Elle caught herself. "Mrs. Scott didn't have friends in Myrtle Beach, did she?"

"According to Mr. Scott, she hated the place. Went once back in the '80s. Swore it was the tackiest place she'd ever been. Nothing but strip malls and fast-food restaurants. She never went back. So, are you one of those reporters?"

"I can promise you I'm not."

"You'll give me your word as a child of God that you aren't?"

"I do," Elle replied, "but I should tell you that I don't know if God would claim me as one of his own."

The woman gave her a curious look. "Spoken like a woman that knows the true value of offering someone their solemn word. Why, then, are you here? And if I don't like the answer, I will be calling the police."

Elle found the woman's intelligence and honesty admirable. She decided to come clean. "I was the one who found Duncan's body on Saturday afternoon. Well, my sister and I were the ones. The twist is that I have some history with Duncan, or at least my extended family does. He was accused of murdering my ex-husband's mother."

Angela's eyes narrowed as she took a deep breath. She took a slow sip of water before setting the glass down and clasping her hands in her lap. "Are you related to the tall fellow with the ponytail?"

"Mid-thirties, brown hair, short temper?" Elle asked.

"Do you know him?"

"That would be my ex-husband's brother, Kelsey. There is no love lost between the two of us."

The woman shook her head and squeezed her hands together event tighter. "He comes by every month or so, drunk as a fiddler. He just sits out in his car, lays on the horn at all hours of the night. He won't leave until the police shoo him away."

"I'm sorry you've had to deal with that."

"I've learned to ignore it. I just keep the doors locked and the police on speed dial. I've been a caregiver most of my life, and every family has its history. There are those stories that my patients will tell me about old flames, friends, neighbors, and family members. I'm usually certain that I'll be the last one to hear these tales.

"Sitting here with Mrs. Scott has felt different, and I can't quite put my finger on it. It's like the story is still being written. Even with Duncan gone and the missus soon to follow, I don't think the story has come to an end yet. As odd and uncomfortable as this has been, I hope I'm here when the final chapter is written."

She took another deliberate sip of water and returned her focus to Elle. "I hope you don't mind me asking, but if you're not looking to cause trouble, what were you hoping to find here?"

Elle stood and returned to the wall of pictures. In one sun-bleached snapshot, a young boy with dirty blond hair and brown eyes stood grinning over a birthday cake. It was a moment of joy forever frozen in time, the smiling child unable to anticipate the sadness that would follow.

"After what happened this weekend, I realized that I didn't know much about Duncan's life. He's been a part of my in-laws' history for as long as I've known them, but he was still a blank canvas to me."

"There may not be much to know. I didn't even meet him after he got out. Derrick was doing the overnight on Friday when he showed up. From everything I've heard, Duncan was a quiet, friendly kid. Maybe a little slow but independent enough. I can tell you that all that happened crushed Mr. Scott's will. I came on just before he passed, and even when he passed, he'd swear he never had a grandson. Just breaks your heart."

Elle gave the pictures one last look then glanced over at Mrs. Scott sitting at her window. "I know when there's a crime like he was accused of, the pain just ripples out. The victim's family is forever changed. At the same time, the family of the accused is never the same. I suppose I just wanted to know who he was and where he had come from."

"Not much left to see here," the woman replied.

Elle thanked Angela for her time and trust. As she turned back under Highway 74, she wondered what would happen to the invalid woman in the wheelchair, now that she was the last Scott standing.

8

The truth of anything at all doesn't lie in someone's account of it. It lies in all the small facts of the time.

— Josephine Tey

Just past noon, Elle pulled into Peg Kinnear's suburban driveway on Selkirk Drive. A 1970s approximation of a Colonial-era original, the facade boasted louvered shutters, wrought iron carriage lights, and a two-story front porch with an ornamental balcony. The paint had cracked and worn in several places, and the shutters faded from forest to moss green. The landscaping was sparse, but Elle could see the lawn was well kept. Behind the house, a large, tree-canopied lot stretched back and abutted the wooded area northwest of St. Andrews.

Elle had seen the house a few times and only from the outside. The homes here were tasteful and, by today's standards, modest but otherwise unremarkable. During their marriage, Dan had been reluctant to visit the house next door, the site of his mother's murder. Despite his younger brother still occupying the Mackay homestead, Dan insisted they meet for family gatherings somewhere else. Anywhere else, really.

Elle imagined the picturesque row of homes on either side of the quiet street as another image trapped in a previous era. There was once money here, she thought. Not in excess but enough to live comfortably. Today, the neighborhood stood as a quiet testament to former middle-class glory.

Before she could pull the key from the ignition, the front door opened, and Peg stepped out onto the small brick portico. Dressed in a frayed men's shirt and worn jeans, she had her short hair held back with a red kerchief. Peg pulled off a pair of yellow gloves and tossed them to one side of the porch, waving Elle up with a bare hand.

Elle closed the SUV's door and waved back. "Good afternoon, Peg," she called out with her warmest smile.

"Hey there, Elle," the older woman replied as she led Elle into the front room. "I wasn't expecting your call this morning, but I'm happy to see you. Sadly, though, Monday is always chore day."

"I won't take up much of your time, Peg. Despite everything, it was good seeing you this weekend."

The woman raised both hands and shook her head. "Wasn't that just the worst thing? I knew the whole episode wasn't going to end well, but... I just couldn't imagine *that*."

The living room dovetailed with the home's exterior. Out of style but well-kept furnishings dotted a formal space that probably saw very little use. Magazines already several years out of date were stacked neatly next to amber glass ashtrays, French provincial-style lamps, and simple arrangements of plastic flowers.

"Why don't we go in the kitchen?" Peg asked. "There's much more light in there. So, tell me, Elle. What did you need to talk to me about?"

Elle took a chair at the Formica kitchen table and set her leather folio at her seat. The room smelled of pine cleaner and coffee. On the center of the table, a glazed orange cake sat half-eaten on a covered glass cake stand.

"I've been thinking about everything that happened Saturday," Elle began with a carefully practiced approach.

"Haven't we all? Coffee? How about a slice of orange cake? Enora Johnson brought it over. I've never cared for it, but I don't mind saving it for company."

"I'm fine, but I thank you. I was talking to Dan last night, and that got me off on a tear."

"How is Dan doing?"

"He's well enough. He's a strong person, and he's got Paige to keep an eye on him."

Peg took the chair across from Elle and took a long, slow sip of coffee. Her eyes regarded her visitor over the rim of the ceramic mug. "So, what was your thought?"

"You probably know better than most, but this is the kind of thing that will be all over the papers. Not just here, but across the country. What happened to Shona was horrible enough, but with Duncan thrown into the mix, it will be a feeding frenzy. As soon as this hits the news, we'll have reporters from God only knows where coming to town and writing about Shona and Duncan and all of us."

Peg set down her mug and nodded her head. "So true. After Shona's death—excuse me, her murder—it was a tempest of writers and news crews. They were stalking us from behind trees and bushes. I couldn't leave my front door without being hounded for a statement or asked about some horrible detail I might have left out. It was just unbearable for me."

"I can only imagine. You know, I am a writer, and we're both practically members of the family," Elle assured her gently, holding Peg's gaze to make her point. "We need to stay ahead of this and handle it between us family and friends. If the story is going to be told, I don't want that slapped together by an outsider."

Peg nodded eagerly. "Well, Elle, I'm happy to help, particularly for you because you're so close to Dan. Anything at all that I can do for him and Kelsey, just ask."

Elle opened her leather folio and withdrew a pen. "Of course, Dan has told me everything, so I have his full side of the story. That's just one perspective, though. Now, Peg, you were so integral to everything that happened that morning. I wanted to talk to you first."

Elle thought she could see the older woman blush. "That is so kind, Elle. Where should I begin?"

"When did you first meet Shona? Just start there."

Peg drummed her fingers on the Formica surface and appeared lost in thought. It was several moments before she spoke.

"Well, she moved in maybe nine or ten years ago. We hit it off immediately. I had lived here for only two or three years myself, so it was nice to have someone else to talk to who wasn't from St. Andrews. It seems like everyone else was born and raised here on Eagle Island."

Elle understood the woman's sense of alienation. The island was a tight-knit community, and even something as simple as Peg's slight outer island accent could set her apart from her Eagle Island-born neighbors.

As the older woman paused, Elle lifted the folio and made an effort to suggest she was taking copious notes. Peg appeared to be encouraged by the gesture.

"It must have been nice having her as a new neighbor," Elle prodded.

"It was nice to have another woman my age here on Selkirk. Before Shona, it was really just me and Orna Gunn across the street. Of course, Dan and Kelsey were always coming and going, so that made things a little more lively here on the edge of town."

"Didn't Shona work for you at one point?" Elle asked. While Dan had rarely spoken of his mother's death, he had been forthcoming with a few facts about her life.

"Oh, yes. She was always so good with numbers. She was a little unsophisticated and far too sentimental, but she knew her math. Not long after I moved here, I married Kirkland Kinnear. Before that, I was just Elizabeth Garrish from Down East.

"When Kirk and I met, though, it was love at first sight. He was so tall, so handsome. But he was hopeless in business. For many years, Kirk & the Tartans was the only proper bar in St. Andrews. I still don't know how he survived all those years—probably just due to its popularity. Kirk never once actually read a bill before either paying it or just ignoring it completely."

"Did Shona help him with that?"

"At first, I tried to, but I was also so busy with the bar. I had taken over all the ordering and the staff. All Kirk had to do was show up and pour drinks, which is what the customers loved so much about the place. I was good at the books, but I was spread too thin. When Shona moved in next door, Kirk was just crazy about her. With her head for figures, we brought her on to do our bookkeeping."

"I remember when the bar burned," Elle replied. "That was one most of us won't forget."

Peg gave her head a small shake. "That was a series of sad events. Just one right after the other." She sighed for a moment. "The bar, however, is a tale for a bit later.

"As for Shona, I'll never forget the day she died. I was going to have Orna Gunn over for coffee. You know Orna— the stout, chatty woman from the city's licensing office. Like I said, she lives right across the street in the modern pink house. We were planning a block party or something, and she and I always ended up in charge of everything."

Peg fidgeted in her seat for a moment and centered her coffee mug in front of her on the table. She turned it a few times to square the handle. To Elle, she appeared lost in thought.

"My biggest regret of my life is that I had rung up Duncan Scott and asked him to take care of a few jobs around the house while Orna and I were talking. He had always been odd but never violent." Peg let out a deep sigh. "I guess hindsight is truly twenty/twenty."

"There's no way you could have known what was going to happen," Elle offered reassuringly.

"Thank you, dear. Well, that morning was in no way unusual. I remember Grier Hammond, the realtor, stopped by to say hello to Shona. In fact, I was watering the plants on my front pizer and saw them say goodbye. Then, Grier drove off. So odd to think that she might be the last person to ever speak to Shona alive."

Elle continued to write. After a pause, she asked, "When did Duncan arrive?"

"Oh, it must have been right around 11 a.m. Duncan showed up at my back patio door, probably just walked down from his farm. It's a few miles, but he never went anywhere but on foot. At the same time, Orna knocked up front. I got Orna set up with coffee in the kitchen and took Duncan to the far side yard to trim back a holly tree that was dropping leaves in the fishpond."

Elle tapped the pen on the pad. "Did he work for you often?"

"Heavens no, just once a month or so. Usually, it was picking up trash or fixing a leaky faucet."

"And Orna?"

"Oh, yes. Orna and I talked for about an hour over coffee and pastries. She was her usual helpful, cheerful self. Always talking a good game and taking on more than she could manage but doing it with a smile. She was getting up to leave, and she asked where Duncan had gone off to. We went and checked the side yard, but Duncan weren't there."

"There was no sign of him?" Elle asked.

"None. And I realized the holly tree hadn't been trimmed. I started calling out for him and only then noticed the back door on the Mackay house was slid open. I called out again to no answer. When I looked inside Shona's back den, I saw her." The woman gave a long pause, her eyes focused on the memory. "She was tied to a chair in the middle of the room. It didn't even occur to me to check if she was still alive. Sometimes, you just know these things by looking."

"That must have been an unimaginable shock."

"Well, I started screaming and ran back to my house. Orna and I locked ourselves in my bedroom and called the police. It was truly a nightmare. I should say that it was the start of a longer nightmare."

"Just the beginning?" Elle realized that she was sitting forward in her chair, her body language suggesting an eagerness for every detail. She coaxed herself back into her seat, relaxing her shoulders as best she could.

"It was the start of a very sad, dark time in my life. First Shona died, then I found out that the bar wasn't as wildly successful as Kirk had led me to believe. I didn't know it at the time, but we were a matter of months from going under. Then a few weeks later, the bar burned to the ground with Kirk inside it."

"I remember when that happened. Did they ever determine a cause?"

"I think they decided that both Kirk and the bar were the victims of an accident. He tripped or had some fit while smoking. I always knew those damn cigarettes would kill him one way or another. In my heart, I sometimes worry that he did it intentionally. But I'll never say it aloud. Well, I guess I can now that the insurance company finally settled."

Elle nodded sympathetically. "How long did that take?"

"Almost five years. I've been scrimping all these years, paying for attorneys, and trying to get by. We just settled earlier this year. You know, Elle, they say that deaths and bad luck come in threes. After Shona and Kirk, I've been waiting five years for the next bell to toll."

"Do you think Duncan Scott might be that third to end the streak?"

Peg shook her head, took a sip of coffee, and let the moment pass.

"It's possible, but I doubt it."

9

Silence, maiden; thy tongue outruns thy discretion.

— Sir Walter Scott

Ten minutes later, Elle stepped back out onto the portico, her leather folio and two wrapped slices of orange cake in her hands. As Peg retrieved her gloves, closed the front door, and disappeared back into the house, Elle examined the pink mid-century style bungalow across the street for any evidence that someone was home. A small economy sedan sat in the driveway, but she could see no other sign of life. Although the large bay window was draped in gauzy white curtains, no light or movement was visible in the front room.

As Elle unlocked her SUV and set the paper plate of cake on the driver's seat, she thought she saw a slight flutter on the far side of the curtain. Gently closing the door, she crossed the street and stopped at the cheerful, berry-colored front door. A small, inset window fitted with rippled glass gave her no clear view inside the house. A few knocks yielded no response. Elle tore a page from her folio and jotted a quick note, leaving it tucked beneath the mailbox flap.

As she stepped back from the quaint bungalow, her eye again caught what she thought might be movement behind the bay curtains. Stepping to the window, Elle could see nothing but the dimmest outlines of furniture and doorways though the sheer white fabric. She continued around the house, surreptitiously stealing quick peeks into bedrooms and bathrooms. On the far side of the house, Elle could make out a cup of tea still steeping on the kitchen counter, but no other sign of Orna.

Frustrated by the chase, she stepped back around the house and into the street. As she opened her car door, she noticed her bright yellow legal paper note missing from the mailbox. She shook her head. "Nothing to do but wait."

Backing out of Peg's driveway, Elle shifted into drive and turned toward St. Andrews proper. At the first stop sign, a faint, authoritative voice startled her from the back seat.

"Turn left here. Stay calm and keep driving."

For a moment, Elle's heart leapt in her chest. For the first time, she realized how on edge the weekend had left her. After the briefest hesitation, she did as she was told. As she steered out of the turn, she adjusted her rearview mirror down a few inches. On the floor of the back seat lay Orna Gunn, sporting an oversized sun hat and covered by a single, crumpled sheet of newspaper.

"Go down to Hampton Drive and make another left. Then pull into the second parking lot on the right."

"Orna, what are you doing?" Elle asked, now with more humor than surprise.

"Just act natural. Everything will be fine," Orna responded in a loud stage whisper.

Elle sighed and continued to Hampton Drive. After a few uneventful blocks, she slid into a parking spot between Thistle Do Nicely and Elle's favorite dry cleaner. She shifted the car into park. "Orna, we're here. If you wanted a coffee, Peg had a pot on."

The older woman lifted and eased herself to a seated position, surveying the lot and crowded outdoor patio.

Elle had met Orna several times, and the woman lived up to her reputation for dramatic exaggeration. She sighed and decided to play along. "Who are we looking for?"

"Reporters, perhaps. News crews more likely."

Elle gave an exaggerated turn, looking in every direction. "No cameras. No reporters. I think we're safe."

"I can't be too careful," she replied in a low register as she cautiously stepped out of the SUV. "But first, I need a coffee since you ruined my tea. And you're paying."

Thistle Do Nicely was always, Elle thought, perfectly named. It always did nicely. A classic British tearoom with a brighter, more modern aesthetic, she found it the perfect place for a midday break. Despite the tight cluster of tables, the constant rabble of voices made private conversation surprisingly easy.

Elle watched with fascination as Orna fussed over her frothy drink. The older woman topped the thick layer of foam with three packets of artificial sweeteners, never stirring them into the coffee below. She added two ice cubes and a long biscotti, pushing the cup to the side of the table.

"Needs time to blend," she explained in a conspiratorial tone. She was dressed in a colorful, silky kaftan emblazoned with jungle designs. Her habit of talking with her hands gave Elle the impression of a large, tropical bird flapping its wings.

Elle found it a curious combination for someone so desperate to avoid undue attention.

"You know, I just happened to be looking out my front window at the exact right moment. I saw you talking to Peg, then you both disappeared for a bit. I didn't recognize you at all, so naturally I assumed you were a reporter. When Shona died, it was an absolute circus. Reporters were *everywhere*, and we were practically celebrities."

"Peg had mentioned that, but—" Elle tried to interject.

"Do you know that I even appeared in an episode of one of those dreadful evening news magazines? It was... what do you call them? A recreation?"

"A reenactment?"

"YES! That's what it was." Her waving hands punctuated her statements with a rattle of bracelets and bangles. "Dreadful. The woman who played me looked *nothing* like me. She was all overemphasis and overacting and flailing of arms and blathering on. You'd think she was auditioning for Shakespeare."

"That must have been difficult for you," Elle offered.

"Terribly. What were we talking about? Oh, this morning. Then, you left me that note and disappeared around the back of my house. I was terrified. I wouldn't put it past one of those *investigator* types to break in for their next scoop. Of course, only then I read your note and recognized you as one of Vee's girls."

"Yes, Orna, Cunningham is my maiden name. We've met several times over the years."

The woman's eyes examined Elle closely, one eyebrow cocked with a look of uncertainty. She dismissed the comment with a wave.

"Well, once it was safe, I knew I had to talk to you, at least be gracious enough to say hello."

"So, you hid in the back of my car?"

"I couldn't risk being seen," Orna replied while clutching two of the three beaded necklaces around her throat. "What if the press had shown up? And they will, I promise you that. Can you hand me a creamer, dear?"

As the older woman scanned the room and windows for the third time, Elle passed her a miniature plastic cup of French vanilla creamer. It soon disappeared into Orna's still-untasted drink. Elle opened her folio and uncapped her pen. She explained her reason for speaking with Peg Kinnear.

Her guest clasped her hands together, her eyes lighting up with a mischievous fire. The response was enthusiastic and immediate. "Of course, I'd be thrilled to help you with such an important project. I can tell you absolutely everything about that horrible morning. I'd do anything for Vee or poor, poor Shona." She paused with a dramatic stare and gently tapped the side of her nose with one finger. "Just please make sure you get the facts right. One more creamer, dear.

"As for me, I've lived in the neighborhood longer than most. My father built that house, you know, and I inherited it from my parents. Back then, we were the last row of houses before you lost yourself in the woods. It was so quiet and pristine in those days. Now, it's nearly impossible to find anything like that on Eagle Island."

Elle watched in bewilderment as Orna added yet another pack of sweetener to the mix, stirring with the nearly dissolved biscotti. She dropped the rest of the dry cookie into the mug and again set the drink aside.

"Then, maybe it was the early '70s, Highlands Construction bought up the final tract and started building those bigger homes across the street. They've run them right up against the tree line. Kirk Kinnear, that was Peg's husband, God rest his soul, moved in perhaps twenty years ago. Peg arrived in St. Andrews about eight years after that, and they were married before she had time to unpack."

The woman leaned in closer to Elle and gave another loud whisper, "Did you know Peg was his third wife? I know no one stays married forever these days, but *three* marriages? It's just beyond the pale. He even asked me out a few times, but I have been very happy with my own little castle. I got the impression, though, that he needed a woman in his life. Some men are just hopeless like that."

Elle nodded enthusiastically. "And Shona?"

"Let's see, Shona moved in only a year or two after Peg and Kirk married. Old Miss Ainsley died, and Shona bought the house. She was already divorced by then, but I suppose she kept the Mackay name. As long as I've known her, it's just been Shona and the two boys."

"And Peg and Shona were close?"

Orna thought for a moment. "Well, I don't know about *close*. They were neighborly enough, seemed to get along fine. I was always closer to Peg, maybe just because she had been there a bit longer. And Shona was a sweetheart—sweetest thing you ever met but not very easy to get to know. She was all about her business and the boys, then Grady Foster for a while before she died."

"What do you remember about that morning?"

Orna added two more sweeteners to her brew and borrowed Elle's spoon to stir for a moment. "I know it was all years ago, but I remember every last detail like it was yesterday. I was going to have lunch with Peg—finger sandwiches, I believe. We needed to go on about the block party that ended up *never* happening because of all the media attention. All that work for nothing.

"A little after breakfast, I was still at home. I happened to notice that Grier Hammond—do you know her? She's *everyone's* realtor. She stopped by to see Shona at just about 9:35, give or take a minute. The mailman—excuse me, it was a mail *lady* then—dropped off the mail while Grier and Shona were still inside. Grier stayed for twelve minutes, not that I was counting. Then she and Shona walked out to Grier's car. I even waved at them from the living room window."

The older woman sighed with exaggerated concern. "You know, I shudder at the thought that I was the last person to see her alive. Well, other than the killer, of course."

"Of course," Elle replied. "Do you remember—"

"At 11:04, give or take a minute, I walked over and knocked at Peg's front door. It took her a few minutes to answer, only because I found out later that Duncan Scott," she touched her chest and said a silent prayer, "had shown up at the same time in back. Peg and I sat down in the kitchen, and I saw Duncan carrying his work bag."

The older woman gasped with a startled yet practiced face. "Elle, do you think that's where he kept his... *kill kit*? I've heard about those on the internet. Every serial killer carries one. That's how you know they are serial killers."

Elle nodded her head and repaid Orna's question with a thoughtful look. "You know, you might be right." She continued nodding and feigned adding a few important notes about kill kits to her notebook.

"Well, Peg took him out back to show him a tree, it was either a dwarf magnolia or a holly tree, I think. Peg came around the patio and into the kitchen. We got down to business planning the block party. And as per usual, Peg made excellent finger sandwiches, but other than that, I did all the heavy lifting.

She loves putting her name on things like this, but I'm the one who's making it all happen."

Elle saw the train going off the track and tried to pull it back on course. "How long did you stay?"

"About an hour later, we were wrapping up. We had five or six of the little egg salad and tuna salad sandwiches left, which Peg suggested we should offer to Duncan. I thought it would be a lovely gesture. She stepped out the back door and called Duncan's name, but he never replied. She walked out of view, and not ten seconds later, I heard her scream. I've never heard such a wail.

"Peg came running back into the kitchen and told me to go check for her pistol in her nightstand. She called 911 in hysterics, then we locked ourselves in her bedroom."

"That must have been such a shock for you." Elle reached out to give her hand a supportive squeeze.

"I can't even begin to explain the pain I felt. It was like Duncan betrayed us all. In one second, we're offering him finger sandwiches, and the next, he's murdered one of our dearest friends." Orna caught herself with a small choke, clutched her chest, and began to cry. Elle couldn't help but notice there weren't any tears.

"Please, don't go on until you're ready," Elle offered.

Orna raised one finger and gave a deep breath. "It must be told. At the time, Peg didn't give me many details. She was too deep in shock, as I think any of us would be. Fortunately…" the woman paused as she caught her own word. "Coincidentally, my niece was a 911 dispatcher at the time, so she was able to fill in a few of the blanks for me."

"Such as?"

"It's just too horrible, but Shona was tied to a chair in the middle of her den. Her hands were tied behind her. Someone had ransacked her bedroom, then strangled her to death. Or perhaps the other way around. In any event, she had been dead for an hour, and Duncan had simply left by the back door and vanished."

As Orna stirred her untasted coffee, Elle thought for a moment. "Before the police arrived, are you sure you hadn't seen anyone else?"

The woman held up her right hand in a show of a solemn oath. "I'd swear to it. Other than Grier and the mail lady, there wasn't a soul on Selkirk Drive. I suppose that someone may have visited coming in through the north woods, but why bother looking?"

She gave her spoon several resolute taps on the side of the mug and returned her coffee to the side of the table.

"There was no doubt Duncan had done it. That evening, they found him hiding in a closet on his grandparents' farm. He had some of poor Shona's jewelry tucked away in that work bag for later. God knows what he needed it for. Probably money for drugs or prostitutes or whatever that kind of lowlife gets up to."

10

A wise man proportions his belief to the evidence.

— David Hume

"So, what did your sleuthing dig up today?" Lana asked as she collected empty dinner dishes from the table. She passed Izzy, who was at odds with the few brussels sprouts still sitting on her plate. The four-year-old was far more interested in getting her aunt's attention by waving her hands.

As Elle handed her sister her own plate, she replied, "Just a few details about the day Shona..." She looked at the twins, both staring back at her in anticipation. "Um... left."

"Ladies?" Sophie's voice came from the kitchen. "Let's save the grown-up talk until their bath time."

"Got it," Lana replied. "Still, we are both worried about Dan. We know you are, too. There's nothing there, and he should be in the clear of Duncan's... problem. But people have been convicted of less."

Elle nodded. "Too true, and I'm worried that Duncan may be another excellent example of that. He may not have been the one who... did that to Shona."

Sophie appeared in the kitchen doorway and took the stack of plates from her wife. "OK, you two win. I'll finish this up and get them in the bath. Go talk this out. And you've got dishes, Elle. Agreed?"

As she closed her home office door, Lana turned to her little sister. "What's this about Duncan? You are really poking a hornet's nest with this one."

"It's just a thought I had," Elle replied as she sank into the loveseat that dominated the picture window overlooking the backyard.

"Your thoughts get you into trouble, baby girl."

"I count on it. It's nothing I can put into words yet, but I've got the feeling that Duncan may not be as guilty as everyone wants to believe he is. The crime simply doesn't fit who he is. In some ways, it's too spur of the moment, and in other ways, it's too premeditated."

"And?" Lana asked, motioning for her sister to continue.

"And what?" Elle replied.

"I know you." She tapped her little sister on the top of the head. "There's something else rattling around in there."

Elle shrugged and gave the slightest roll of her eyes. "And… we know that someone killed Duncan and is trying to focus some blame on Dan. Maybe someone else did the same thing to Duncan. Maybe he was just a convenient patsy instead of a spree killer."

Lana leaned back in her leather desk chair and put her hands behind her head. "Ellie, I'm your biggest fan. On this one, though, I think you're spinning your wheels. Don't waste your energy on all these tangents. You've got to focus on what's important. Just keep Dan in the clear. Do that, and you've done your good deed for the day."

"But Lana, what if I'm right? If someone was targeting both Dan and Duncan, then the two murders must be connected. If someone framed Duncan, we saw what happened to him. Now, if they're implicating Dan, he might be a target. That scares the hell out of me."

The older Cunningham sister rubbed her fingers through her hair and leaned forward as though to emphasize a minor surrender. "Listen, Ellie, I know contract law, not criminal law. So, I'm probably not the best person to bounce this off of. That prosecutor I talked to on Saturday, the one that owes me a few favors, he was working with one of the original prosecutors on Duncan's case. Let me see if I can give him a call for you. Trey's a sharp lawyer and a stand-up guy."

Before Elle could answer, a polite knock echoed from the hallway. Sophie's voice came through the door. "Elle, you've got a visitor."

Elle and Dan sat on the white-slat porch swing as he gently rocked it with his feet. The evening sky had begun turning from purple to dark blue, although the stars had yet to come out. Across the yard, neon pinpoints flashed and swayed in the twilight as lightning bugs began their dance. The coming night was cool and calm, a welcome respite from the past few days.

"I tried texting you a couple of times today," he said.

"Sorry. I was doing work research all afternoon. I never looked at my phone," she lied. Despite her desire to help, Elle found herself feeling guilty about the questions she was asking. She didn't like to go behind Dan's back, but this way, she reasoned, might hurt less in the end.

"Just like old times." He gave a halfhearted laugh. "I just wanted to say thanks again for the assist yesterday. I was going to call Kelsey, but I'm glad you were there instead."

"Always will be," she replied. She thought for a moment and reconsidered her tactics. A little honesty, she thought, might be a better approach. "Dan, can I ask you a difficult question?"

"Just one?"

"Might be two or three."

His feet stopped the rocking motion of the swing. "Is it about Mom?"

"Yeah. It is."

"I need to know why." His voice was defensive, but Elle realized he was still talking. This was further than they usually got during a difficult conversation.

"I'm worried about you. More, I'm worried that someone may want to hurt you or at least make you look like something you're not. You know how I follow my gut. Right now, it's telling me there's something going on, something else that we aren't seeing."

Dan thought for a moment then continued rocking the swing. As if on cue, a breeze came through the porch with the scent of night blooming jasmine.

"What do you want to know?"

"Anything you want to tell me. Anything that just doesn't make sense."

"Ellie, none of it makes any sense. For as long as I can remember, it was just me and Mom and Kelsey. Dad left before Kelsey was born, so Mom did whatever was needed to make sure we were happy and fed. She was a good woman and a kind soul. There's no reason for anyone to ever have hurt her."

"Can you tell me about her?" Elle asked. "In all the time we were together, I realize I don't know much of anything about her. I wish I did."

"Well, she didn't have any family. Both of her parents died in an accident of some sort over on the East Coast when she was young. She never spoke about them. So, when Dad dipped, she went to work doing her bookkeeping. We all lived in Fayetteville for a long time, then she got her job here, so she moved. Kelsey and I didn't have anything tying us down then, so we came with her, and I brought Paige." He let his voice trail off.

"What about the time everything happened?" Elle asked in a gentler tone.

"Hmmm," he paused and thought. "At the time, Paige and I were first living in our house on Juniper. Kelsey had just moved back in with Mom maybe the week before. He and his girlfriend then, I think it was Molly—Molly Blake, I think—were staying in the master bedroom, and Mom had moved to the guest room with the single bed. Then, Mom died, and everything just fell apart.

"Honestly, when I saw Duncan this weekend, it wasn't even anger for me. Most days, I take a big step back and see what these twins have—two amazing parents, an aunt who loves them, your mom, Sophie's parents, the whole family package. I want that for Paige, and Duncan took what little she had away from her. She's just got me. No mother, no grandparents, an uncle of very questionable value as a role model, and not much else. I don't want her growing up alone. She deserves so much more."

"Dan, she's got you," Elle replied. "And us. She will never be alone." For the next several minutes, the pair sat in silence and watched the fireflies scribble on the night sky.

11

There is no sunlight in the poetry of exile.

— H. V. Morton

"Ellie, when are you going to get a house like this?" Vee pointed out the SUV window as Elle pulled up along the Juniper Street curb. The home was a compact, well-kept one-story in a classic Southern red brick style. She parked behind a beat-up Chevy truck and left the engine running.

"Mama, I had a house like this. If you remember, I had *this* house when I was married to Dan."

"So, why don't you get one of your own and give your sister a little space."

"I'm working on it, Mama," Elle replied. She had answered the same question a dozen times in the past few weeks. She knew the script by heart. "And yes, my new job pays enough, but I want to have a good down payment before I commit to a mortgage."

"You know they'd probably pay you better if you actually went into the office now and then."

Elle muttered something under her breath as she turned the car off. She reconsidered and restarted the engine to keep the AC running.

"They'd probably pay you even better if you didn't mumble," her mother admonished her. "No one can understand you when you mumble."

She thought better of it and turned the engine off again. "Just be a minute, Mama. Crack a window if it gets hot."

"Ellie, dear, the windows are electric and don't work unless the key—" Elle missed the rest of her mother's advice as she shut the SUV door behind her.

Coming up the front walk, Elle paused as the screen door flew open. A tall, lanky man in his early thirties stormed from the front hall, slamming the rickety frame behind him. He pointed at Elle with one finger and came to a quick stop.

Kelsey Mackay bore more than a passing resemblance to his older brother. Taller by a few inches, the younger of the two was leaner, as though nature had started with twins but stretched one just a bit too much. His long, dark brown hair was pulled back in a ponytail, and his beard had a bushy fullness that obscured his mouth.

"Morning, Kelsey," Elle offered. "You looking for me?"

"I wasn't. I was looking for Dan, but you're on my list," he snapped in a hoarse voice. He glared down at her, his body coiled and jittery as though waiting for the right moment to lash out. Where Dan usually succeeded with quiet stoicism, Elle thought, Kelsey made do with anger and thinly veiled threats.

"Well, you found me."

"I'm just gonna say this one time. You leave my mother alone. Got it?" With each word, he jabbed his finger in Elle's direction. "I never liked you to begin with, but now you're really pissing me off. Mom's gone, and you're trying to get her murderer off the hook. That bastard is dead, Elle. Nothing's gonna change that, and nothing is bringing Mom back. Back the hell off."

Before she could answer, Kelsey pushed past her, nearly knocking her off the path. In eight long strides, he was in his truck. He pulled away with a squeal of balding tires, leaving Elle to watch him speed off.

"Uncle Kelsey says hi," Paige said from the front door, "and some other stuff."

Elle blinked and looked from Paige to the street and back to Paige. "Um, I wasn't expecting that this morning. You still up for some shopping? We've got a couple of errands to run for Mama but thought we'd get some lunch on the way."

"Sure," the girl replied with a shrug. "Let me get some stuff for my chickens." A few minutes later, the three women were turning toward the All in a Row office off Main.

"What was all that awful racket back at the house?" Vee asked from the back seat, not for the first time.

"Mama, let it go. Kelsey and I have never gotten along," Elle replied. "He was just really feeling it today."

"Oh, it was more than that," Paige offered from the passenger seat. Elle sighed and focused on the road ahead. "Uncle Kelsey is pissed off—"

"Language."

"Sorry, Uncle Kelsey is very, very upset with Aunt Elle. He was looking for Daddy, but he was already headed out to work."

"Well, Lord knows that could be any of a hundred things," Vee scoffed with an exasperated huff. "What is it this time?"

"Somebody called him and said that Aunt Elle was trying to prove that the Duncan guy was innocent. Even though it's obvious to everyone else that he's guilty, she is trying to get him off Scot free."

"That's not true," Elle replied. "I'm just worried about your dad. And if what happened to your grandmother is part of all this, then I want to know the whole story. Nothing more and nothing less."

"So, why do they call it 'Scot free'?" Paige asked. "Is it like a *Braveheart* thing or something?"

Elle smiled and continued to drive. "Do you want the short answer or the long answer?"

"Um, short answer, please."

"Paige, this is one of those times when language can be a little confusing. When I do my historical research for work, I always have to focus on making sure what words mean now and how it relates to what they meant back then."

"We're getting the long answer," Vee grumbled from the back seat.

"Thank you, Mama. And language is a living thing, so words grow and evolve. Some even die off altogether or change as they pass from one culture to another. For example, remember the little double heart silver pin I gave you last Christmas?"

"The one you called a Luckenbooth?"

"Exactly! Now, that's an old Scottish tradition that started five hundred miles away in Norway."

From the back seat: "Ellie dear, one long winded explanation at a time."

"Right." Elle's voice sped up a tick as she eagerly dove into her wheelhouse: history and language. "So, back to 'Scot free.' It has nothing, in fact, to do with Scotland. The phrase started over a thousand years ago in Scandinavia. A 'skat,' or later a 'scot,' was a payment kind of like a tax. If someone was able to avoid paying that tax, that was considered 'scot free.' Over the centuries, it came to mean anyone or anything that didn't have to pay the proper penalty. If you got away with it, you got off scot free."

Paige looked at her aunt, her mouth hanging open. After a few seconds, she blinked. "Like, how do you know all this? Why do you know all this? Even more important, why are you telling me all this?"

Elle laughed. "Paige, I pretended to pay attention through two hours of you explaining which chicken breed does better in captivity than which other breed. And before that, it was the secrets of proper welding. You can take five minutes of linguistics history."

"And this is important *why*?" Vee prompted her daughter.

"Excellent question, Mama. It's important because how we use language is important. The names we give ourselves and the things around us are important. These words help to define who we are and how we define our world. It's the most central part of our culture."

Paige nodded slowly, then shook her head. "But you didn't answer my question. Why should we keep kicking it around? If this Duncan guy is dead now, and he killed Grandmama, that's like justice served. Isn't it?"

"Ellie, let me handle this one" Vee replied. "Now, Paige, what we think justice is and what justice should be are often two very different things. Justice can be tricky, it can be uncomfortable, and it can even be painful for those we love. Just know that as long as we focus on what's right—not necessarily what's easy—justice always wins in the end, even if we're not around to see it. And in some cases, like this one, justice needs a little push. That's where your Aunt Elle comes in."

As Elle pulled onto Adams Street, Vee pointed at an empty spot. "Ellie, there's an empty spot. Park there."

"That was the plan, Mama."

"I just need to run into the office for one second. Don't leave me."

"Again, that was still the plan, Mama."

As Vee disappeared across the street, Paige turned off her phone and looked up at Elle.

"Sorry about all that. The language stuff was actually kind of neat."

Elle shrugged. "It's OK. The chicken stuff was kind of neat, too. I never knew how much I didn't know about raising backyard poultry."

"Yeah, it's just that I get so excited about something, and I want to learn everything I can about it. Then I want to share it with everybody because it's just so amazing. Dad says it's just part of being a teenager. He thinks I'll grow out of it someday."

"I hope not," Elle replied with a smile.

"So, can you tell me about the Luckenbooth thing later?"

"It's a deal."

As Elle spoke, Vee opened the back door and hopped back in the SUV. A large, flat package wrapped in brown kraft paper and tied with twine stuck out from her shoulder bag.

"What did you get, Miss Vee?" Paige asked.

"It's not polite to ask what a lady has in her purse," Vee reprimanded her gently as she searched for the seatbelt. "But if you must know, it's just scrapbooking supplies."

"How many scrapbooks do you need, Mama?"

"Never you mind, Elle. When you're my age, you've got a lifetime of memories and not always the memory to keep up with them. So, are we ready for lunch? Paige, dear, are you still vegetarian?"

"Vegan," the girl replied. "And no, not right now. But I still don't like wearing leather."

"Well, then, no leather for lunch, but everything else is still on the menu. Ellie, turn back to Main. All our choices are back that way."

As Elle made the turn, her phone chirped with a message signal.

"Don't touch that phone, Ellie. Not while you're driving," her mother warned. "You're setting a bad example for Paige."

Elle pulled into a parallel spot on Main and retrieved her phone from her pocket. A message from Trey Howard popped up in her notifications. "Elle, it's Trey. Friend of Lana. Time for lunch near the courthouse?" Elle fired off a quick response, and Trey replied in kind.

"Can you two handle lunch without me?" Elle asked.

"We can make it a girls' lunch, can't we, Paige?"

The teen looked up, shrugged, and nodded.

"I'll take that as a yes," Elle replied. "This may only take a few minutes, so I'll join you as soon as I'm done. You like pho, don't you, Paige?"

The girl's eyes lit up. "I love pho."

"Mama, try Pho Real half a block back on the right. I'll be back as soon as I'm done."

The courthouse square where she had met Jonah Tanner sported a weekday addition: a street taco truck with a line of hungry office workers. Elle shielded her eyes from the midday sun as she tried to read the handwritten sandwich board menu.

"What do you like here?" she asked.

"Never had anything at Tacotastico that I didn't like," Trey replied. "Taco Tuesday is one of the only reasons I've liked returning to the office."

Perhaps five or ten years her junior, Trey Howard had a youthful enthusiasm that Elle found magnetic. Just over six feet, she guessed, he wore a well-tailored suit and a lopsided grin. His broad shoulders suggested more athlete than prosecutor, and the blue eyes, Elle had to admit, were a damn nice touch. After ordering a pair of manager's specials, they settled under a tree to wait for their lunch.

"Listen, I don't think there's anything legally wrong with me discussing the Scott case, but I'd appreciate you leaving my name out of this," he began. "It's all a matter of public record at this point, but still the optics are important when you're playing the political game."

"Understood," Elle replied. "And thanks again for taking me up on my questions. I feel bad that Lana had to burn through her favor for me."

Trey laughed. "This one is on the house. Honestly, you're something of a local legend around the courthouse. I mean most of us were familiar with your name after your, well, let's call them misadventures. But after all that crap that went down on Roan Island, you're the woman of the year. Easiest murder—excuse me, easiest five murders I've ever had to handle. You tied that one up before my office had time to unlock our front door. The only downside is you may have shown up Detective Tanner. You're making his job look too easy."

"Jonah can handle himself. Plus, like you said, it was less work for all of you."

The small black pager buzzed in Trey's hand. "One sec, be right back with lunch." Two minutes later, they were both talking around mouthfuls of seafood tacos with black beans and chorizo.

"Elle, before we start, let me give you some ground rules. I've already heard about the questions you've been asking.

Orna Gunn is my aunt by marriage, and she has never met a secret she wanted to keep. She told me about the book, and I think that's all fine and dandy."

"But?"

"Yup, there's a 'but.' The DA has no interest in reopening the Scott case, and I think that's where you're heading. Call it a hunch. Duncan Scott is dead, his victim is still dead, and no one else is asking for another bite at the apple."

"Understood."

"So, what's your angle?" She found she was appreciating his direct approach, and she decided to give it back in kind.

"Just curious about Duncan's death and why Dan was implicated. Simple as that."

"Simple as that," he sounded unconvinced. "I'll give you what I can, and just use it wisely. Agreed?"

"Agreed. What can you tell me about the crime itself?"

"Let's see. From memory, I know that the police were called by a pair of neighbors. One or both of them had discovered the body, I can't remember which. I don't think it was Orna, though. I'm sure I'd remember her telling the story. Shona Mackay, the victim, had been strangled and bound to a chair in her den. Scott used a length of paracord from the victim's garage to tie her up. There were no signs of a struggle or any kind of sexual assault. She was just tied and garroted. According to the ME, she had been dead about an hour when the police arrived."

"What about the rest of the house?"

"Well, the guest bedroom had been ransacked in a hurry. A few pieces of jewelry were missing, but we didn't know that until they were recovered from Scott's family farm. I think it was a pair of rings. No prints or DNA on the cord. Just small traces of leather like you'd find on a handyman's work gloves.

The traces were a visual match to a pair of gloves Scott used, but the gloves themselves were never recovered.

"Let's see. Only prints of any value were a handprint left by Scott on the sliding glass door. The handle had been wiped clean. There were no other prints or DNA that shouldn't have been there, and the other doors to the house were locked. No one else was seen entering or leaving the premises all morning per my very observant aunt across the street."

"Since you mentioned Orna, it sounds like she was probably at Peg's house during the time Shona was killed. Did she notice anything else?"

He shook his head. "Nothing that she hasn't already mentioned a hundred times. And I think it would have been impossible for someone else to have come in through the sliding glass door while Scott was working in the yard without him seeing the intruder. Plus, you have to add in the fact that he did virtually none of the work Miss Kinnear requested. He literally walked out, went ostensibly to work, and a short while later just disappeared."

"And that was it?"

"Pretty much. The police arrested Scott at his grandparents' farm that afternoon with two of the victim's rings in his possession. He claims he found her dead but was too scared to call the police, so he fled. Plus, he already had a record, mostly fighting and disorderly conduct. It was by no means an airtight case, but it was enough to secure the plea. I think Scott realized it was a way to stay off death row. We haven't had an execution here in almost twenty years, but the death penalty stays on the table in North Carolina."

Elle picked out the last few pieces of shrimp and chorizo from her lunch and tossed the paper basket in the garbage bin.

"You're right, that was a damn good taco." She thought for a moment more. "What about the problems with his appeal?"

Trey shifted in his seat and appeared to choose his words carefully. "Officially? Officially, now there aren't any problems. With Scott dead, the whole thing just goes away. Off the record? I think it was a combination of an overzealous defense attorney, my former boss as prosecutor, and an old-school judge. Everyone wanted the matter resolved, so they resolved it. Nice and tidy, almost. Then, a fresh-out-of-law-school public defender was looking to make a name for himself and started going through recent convictions. He put two and two together and got five.

"It was going to be a hell of a headache to sort out, but the new judge decided on a home release. Local law enforcement was told to keep an eye on him."

"Yeah, hell of a lot of good that did," Elle noted.

"Can't do nothing but agree with you there," Trey concurred. "And one more thing that I thought might be of interest to you. After Lana reached out, I pulled some of my old boss's notes together and made some calls. During the years that Scott was behind bars, he only ever had one visitor. Not even his grandparents came to see him."

Elle shook her head. "And?"

"Grady Foster. He started visiting Duncan about two years ago. They met almost monthly until he was released."

Elle pulled into an empty loading lane across the street and waved to her mother under the awning at Pho Real. She thought Vee looked disgruntled. She hoped she was wrong.

"Did you get everything you needed, Ellie?" Vee asked from the back seat as they pulled away from the curb.

"I certainly did, Mama. How was the pho?"

"Amazing," Paige gushed, then she paused to look at the older woman beside her. "But I don't think Miss Vee was so into it."

"If I wanted chicken soup, I'd make it myself," Elle's mother said in her most matter-of-fact tone. "I wanted to give the chef a few helpful suggestions on seasoning, but they wouldn't let me near the kitchen. I did, however, enjoy my time with Paige. So, what did you learn?"

"Not a whole lot of anything new, Mama. It was more about seeing if everybody remembered the same thing. It's like when I do my research. Do all the accounts line up? There are the parts everyone can agree on; those are usually safe to accept. It's the differences you need to take a second look at. If one person says A and another says B, why is it? Is it perspective or faulty memory or deception?"

Vee nodded in agreement then waved one hand to catch her daughter's attention. "Ellie, before I forget, Dan called Paige while we were at lunch. He's behind schedule at work, so she's having dinner with the Cunninghams. I called Lana, and all of us are having Chinese food at my house. When we're done with errands, let's visit the ValleyMart then head to my place."

"So, where do we need to go next?" Elle asked.

Paige perked up. "Can we go to the farm and feed store over next to the mall?"

"Sure. Is this something new for your chickens?"

"No, I'm completely over chickens. Everyone is doing it now, and they are a *lot* of work. I just need to talk to the guy about where to sell them and the coop."

"That was quick," Vee commented from the back.

"Yeah, with school and all I don't have time for feeding and cleaning. And I am really, really getting into slam poetry. It's all I think about." She pulled out her phone. "I've got like ten poems I've already written, and I didn't use any swears. Tell me what you think."

In the rearview mirror, Elle caught her mother's eye. She thought she saw terror there.

12

When the heart is full, the tongue will speak.

— Scottish Proverb

Sophie gave her sister-in-law the briefest flash of a smile as she delivered the punchline, "He said 'I forgot her name ten years ago, and I'm afraid to ask.'" She was rewarded with a laugh that was both deep and sincere. Elle reveled in the moments when Sophie let down her guarded demeanor. She put a great deal of stock in being a dentist and a mother of two, and Elle loved seeing the goofy side of her personality slip out from time to time.

"I can't take credit for that one," she continued. "Marc is my new dental hygienist, and he's got a million of them. I'm honestly surprised I remembered the whole thing."

While Lana was certainly the public face of the marriage, Sophie Cunningham-Klein, DDS, brandished a sharp, intuitive wit that only those closest to her got to see. Despite their outward dissimilarities, Elle admired how well the pair came together. Despite being two very different women with two very different personalities, they formed a beautifully matched couple.

The half-filled paper containers and crumpled sauce packets of take-out Chinese food lay scattered across a table that could seat twelve, maybe more. Vee Cunningham's house was large and sprawling, even by St. Andrews' standards. More than forty years of building her own maid service had served her very well. And like her best clients, Vee enjoyed a home that was well appointed, well kept, and spotless.

"Paige has the twins," Lana said, coming down the stairs from the second floor. "Mama is taking a nap, so it's just us girls. What did your fortune say, Ellie?"

She broke open the brittle shell and squinted. "'Hard work pays off in the future, laziness pays off now.' Nope, I want a do-over." She tossed the slip of paper and searched the table for an unopened cookie. "Here we go. 'You learn from your mistakes... you will learn a lot today.'"

"I think that's actually worse," Sophie commented with a snicker.

Taking a seat at the table, Lana ate the cookie her sister had discarded. "So, Ellie, what mistakes did you make today?"

"I can tell this is going to be over my pay grade," Sophie added as she rose from the table. "I'm making coffee. Anyone else want a cup?" Her wife raised a hand while Elle shook her head.

Lana turned her attention back to her sister. "OK, baby girl, I'll let you off the hook. You were as quiet as a church mouse during dinner. So, you were either sleeping with your eyes open, or you've got something on your mind. I'm guessing it's the second one. What did you come up with?"

Elle stretched and leaned back in her chair, finishing the last piece of broken cookie. "Well, Trey was an angel, and a damn good-looking one at that. He didn't give me anything earth-shattering, but he certainly went above and beyond. Did I mention his looks?"

Lana laughed and held up two fingers. "That's twice. Let's focus. What have you stitched together?"

"Just a few pieces here and there. Still, though, I feel like I'm missing something bigger. Everything right now is just a hunch."

"And what about Duncan's murder has got you hunching?"

"It's not Duncan, it's Shona," Elle admitted with a groan. She tucked her hands behind her head and began to knead the back of her neck. "The way everyone says it happened doesn't make sense."

"Do murders ever really make sense?"

"Not on the surface, but there's got to be a certain logic to the crime. For most of us, it's an act of last resort. You try everything else, then you end up killing—either by accident or with premeditation."

"And which was it for Duncan?" Lana smiled as Sophie brought her a large mug of heavily creamed coffee.

"If this is more murder talk, I'll be in the kitchen starting some brownies for family day at Simon's class tomorrow. You didn't forget, did you, Lana?"

"How could I forget family day?" Lana asked as Sophie moved toward the kitchen.

Leaning across the table to her sister, she whispered, "I totally forgot family day." She gave her broadest smile. "And I guarantee Sophie heard that."

"Sure did, babe," came from the kitchen.

"Love you, too," Lana replied with an eyeroll and a smile. "OK, my marriage is safe as houses, so let's get back to Shona. What's in your head?"

"Trey gave me more of the details of the actual crime. Most of it doesn't necessarily point to Duncan."

"Such as?"

Elle leaned forward, dropping her tone to spare Sophie any unnecessary details. "She was tied up with cord from her locked garage. If Duncan had planned all this out, why would he stop and look for something to tie her up with once he got to the house? What's he going to do, just walk through, say 'Hey, don't mind me, just looking for something to kill you with,' and proceed down the hall? I doubt it."

Lana nodded slowly then shrugged. "Good point. Maybe he had picked it up on an earlier trip?"

Elle dismissed the suggestion with a shake of her head. "Duncan didn't come across as someone with skill at long-range planning. Everyone seems to agree it was a crime of opportunity or passion, so it's hard to assume he'd plan that one piece during a visit a month or two earlier."

"Point well taken. I'm not convinced, but I'm open," Lana said with thoughtful enthusiasm.

"Second, how would he keep her quiet while he was tying her up? Peg and Orna would have been, what, fifty or sixty feet away? Shona hadn't been struck, so she likely wasn't knocked out. Is she just going to sit patiently while he secures her to the chair when her next-door neighbor is within easy earshot?"

Lana went still for a moment, her eyes focused on a distant thought before she motioned her sister to continue.

Elle gave a quick smile; she knew she was getting through to her big sister. "Then there are his fingerprints. Or rather, his handprint. Most everything was wiped down except the big handprint on the glass door. Why did he break in, then put his gloves on to kill Shona?"

As Lana squinted in thought, Elle knew she had taken a step or two back. "Like you said, baby girl, he's not the big thinker. Maybe the gloves didn't occur to him until he was tying her up. Maybe he cleaned up after himself and forgot the glass door. It's not outside the realm of possibility."

Elle nodded as her sister sipped her coffee. "Those I can give you. It could be coincidence or just poor execution on his part. There's one more piece that just doesn't fit. Shona had just moved from the master bedroom to the guest room. Kelsey and his girlfriend had been staying with her for maybe the past week. Why did the killer only search the guest room and not the master bedroom? Even if it was Duncan, he'd have gone through what he thought was her room. That would logically be where she kept her jewelry."

Lana set the mug down and paused before speaking. Elle could see the wheels turning, trying to find an explanation for facts that didn't fit the crime as it had been portrayed. "Maybe he tied her up, then she told him where to find her jewelry just to try and keep him happy—"

Elle spat out her response before her sister could finish. "I don't buy it. If she could take enough breath to explain it to him, she could also scream for help."

Lana swirled her mug and furrowed her brow as her eyes grew sharp. "I get where you're coming from, Elle. I really do. But so far, nothing else makes any sense. The one thing I've always heard about Shona is that she was an angel. Why would anyone want to kill her? If not for those rings, then what? At the same time, I'm not going to tell you you're wrong. Your heart is in the right place, and you've always had a good gut for stuff like this."

Elle laughed. "My gut has gotten me in a lot of trouble."

"Yeah, but you're learning. Getting better every day. So, what's it telling you now?"

"Thanks, Lana. Right now? It's saying that something is very, very wrong, something I'm not seeing. I don't have the 30,000-foot view, so I'm still stumbling around in the weeds. My only hope is that whatever happened in the past doesn't come back to hurt Dan or Paige in the future. I will promise them both that."

"Did Trey give you anything else?"

Elle snickered. "Well, he gave me a warm feeling, followed quickly by a sad feeling that maybe I'm turning into a cougar."

Lana burst out laughing. "Good grief, you're not even forty yet. I think Trey is maybe thirty-three or thirty-four. That's not exactly robbing the cradle. This is the twenty-first century."

"Actually, that is comforting."

"And I agree, he's damn easy on the eyes, but I don't think you two would work out."

Elle wrinkled her nose and shot her sister a playfully sour look. "What makes you so sure?"

"Baby girl, you know he plays for my team, right?"

"Lana, how'd you put it? This *is* the twenty-first century. You can just say he's gay."

"Ellie, he's on my *team*. He actually plays for my co-ed softball team, the Eagle Island Eagles."

"Original name. Why am I just now hearing about this?"

Lana leaned back in her chair, spreading her arms in mock aggravation. "Just? I've been begging you to come to a game for three years. But every time, it's an excuse. 'I've got jury duty again.' 'I'm too hungover to breathe.' 'I just woke up and I'm not sure where I am.' 'I just pushed my husband and his floozy into a ditch.' 'I'm stuck in county lockup for a couple of days.' 'I'm marooned on an island investigating my old boyfriend's murder.' If you're going to make up excuses, let's try and keep them believable."

"OK, the jury duty one was a lie," Elle deadpanned.

Lana tilted her head and raised an eyebrow. "Ellie, I know. We only play on Saturdays."

"OK, but you never once told me you and Trey both play in the same league."

"Same team, but he's in a totally different league. He's our golden boy at shortstop. I'm a disaster on first base, just there because of my reach. We'd be a complete dumpster fire without him. With him, we're just a train wreck."

"I've never actually seen you play, but I always imagined you'd be pretty good."

"Naw, volleyball was always my jam. According to Sophie, I'm just there as the eye candy. And she thinks it's good to let the twins know that even Mommy can lose—a lot and often—and that's OK."

"So, Trey is really that good?"

"Yeah, and his husband is a beast of a pitcher."

"So, gay?"

"Husband. Yup. That's how gay works."

"You could have just led with that. Saved us all this crap about 'Who's on first.'"

"Baby girl, I just told you. I'm on first. Plus, this was way more fun."

From the dining room, Elle could hear Sophie laughing in the kitchen.

13

As I grow older, I pay less attention to what men say. I just watch what they do.

— Andrew Carnegie

As the sun rose over the Cape Fear River to the east, Elle lay in bed and flipped through her mental notes. Just beyond the slivers of morning light that slipped through the wooden blinds, she pictured Shona Mackay, bound and lifeless, tied to a dining room chair. In her mind's eye, she searched that room she had only visited two or three times, looking for any clue as to what had happened to this beloved mother and friend.

She replayed pieces and parts of her recent conversations, trying to create a reliable narrative of what had happened that horrible morning. In some moments, she had a clear picture of where the players were positioned, their actions and intentions. In others, she understood virtually nothing. She knew that filling these gaps was her goal.

Just finishing her fifth review of her time with Trey Howard, she jumped with a start as her cell phone buzzed on the nightstand. It was a local number but one she didn't recognize.

"Good morning?" she answered with a bit of hesitancy.

"Hey there, is this Elle Cunningham?" a boisterous yet authoritative voice replied.

"Close enough. I married into the Mackays a few years back."

"Sorry, my mistake, but that makes a little more sense. Grier Hammond here, Realtor with Sage Palm Properties. Did I wake you?"

Elle sat up straight in bed, tucking a few stray strands of hair behind her ears. "Grier, no not at all. I'm just surprised to get your call. I've been thinking about you."

"Well, Orna Gunn called me yesterday and gave me an earful about your secret book project. And I don't know if you can tell, but I'm making air quotes around the 'secret' part."

Elle gave a soft chuckle as she slipped out of bed. "It was implied."

The woman on the other end gave a deeper laugh. "I have known that woman for years and never known her once to keep a secret. It's like that bus in that movie. She's worried that if she ever stops talking, she'll explode."

Elle thought it was a perfect analogy. "So, what can I do for you, Ms. Hammond?"

"Grier is fine. Is Elle OK with you?"

"Of course."

"Between other unnecessary and unsolicited bits of gossip, Orna let slip that you might want to talk to me about what happened to poor Shona Mackay. So, did you marry Dan or the other one?"

"Dan. It didn't stick, but we're still in touch. And yes, I'd love to talk to you if you have the time."

"Elle, I'm a real estate procurement professional. All I do is talk and make time. If you're here in St. Andrews, I can meet you at my office. I'm on Main in the Dunmark Building."

"I know exactly where that is. Give me thirty minutes to get there?"

"Looking forward to it, and please say hello to your mother for me."

Half an hour later, Elle sat in her SUV on a narrow side street just off Main. From her secluded parking spot, she finished a warm oat muffin and a cold cup of apple juice. Tossing the muffin wrapper into the back seat, she gathered her folio, stepped onto the street, and turned toward the address she had been given.

Even at this early hour, the locals and tourists thronged the central avenue of St. Andrews. A new sidewalk breakfast café bustled with happy customers while neighboring merchants unlocked their doors and set out clapboards or rolling racks of colorful summer wear.

Elle passed a hand-lettered sign in gilt on dark green marking the historic Dunmark Building. Dating from the mid-1800s, the two-story Classical Revival former mansion was dominated by a series of large, wood-grilled windows surrounded by white stuccoed brick. Since her childhood, Elle had regarded the Dunmark as the shining example of old-world Southern architecture. She imagined it as something both of a particular era and, at the same time, ageless.

Passing through the trellised gate, she crossed a small front courtyard, letting her fingers trail through the cool water of the bubbling central fountain. She entered the building's front hall and found Sage Palm Properties' door just inside on the right. She tried the knob without success and gave a quick knock.

The woman that greeted Elle perfectly matched the voice she had first heard that morning. Grier Hammond was a well-preserved sixty-five or so with a fashionable wedge cut and an eclectic, curated style. From the first moment, she radiated warmth and professionalism, greeting Elle with a firm handshake and a photo business card.

Her office suited her to a tee. Large windows flooded the tastefully appointed seating area with a warm glow while leafy, natural plants softened the room's sharp lines and stark white palette. With both her host's personality and surroundings, Elle felt immediately at home.

"I'm sure we've met somewhere on the island," Grier began. "Didn't you go to the Roan Island Games with your mother? Vee Cunningham, right?"

"That would be me," Elle replied.

"So, what are you up to now?"

"Long story, but I'm working for Coira Buchanan-Berman. I conduct demographic and historical research for her firm."

"Coira's a good friend. Known her for ages. If you don't mind my professional curiosity, are you living here or over in Wilmington?"

"Mostly here. I'm a recent returnee; I've been bouncing around here and there. Now that I'm back, I'm staying with my sister and her family for a bit."

"Well, anything you need, let me know. I can find you a place that's perfect and below market before the listing even goes wide." Grier smiled and handed Elle a second business card. "Funny story, but I sold your mother the house over off Douglas. It was one of the first sales I ever made."

"That's the house I grew up in. Mom still lives there. In fact, we all had dinner at the house last night."

"Well, when it's the right house, it's the right house. I've always been so damn proud of her. From day one, I knew she was a go-getter, but I've never seen someone grow a business like she has. Your mother has got one hell of a knack for making money."

Grier motioned her to the seating area where she took a wide, leather easy chair by the window. Elle selected the white and floral couch, setting her shoulder bag and folio beside her.

"So, what can I do for you and your 'secret' book? Orna gave me only the broadest, most breathless details." She gave Elle a smile and wink that warmed the younger woman like a summer morning. It was no surprise that Grier excelled as a salesperson; Elle envied her innate knack for building an instant rapport.

"To keep this short, I've been doing research on Shona, and it all came to a head this weekend."

The older woman whistled. "I heard about that. My team was doing a showing over in the Historic District. Saturdays are usually my busy days with open houses and all. Of course, St. Andrews society being what it is, I had heard about Duncan Scott before lunch. News like that doesn't stay on people's tongues too long."

"What can you tell me about Shona?"

"I don't know that there's much to tell. I've gone over that day a thousand times in my mind, and I always come up empty. I sold Shona her house when she had moved here from someplace a little further inland. We had talked a few times about her helping out with my accounting, but nothing ever came of it."

"Peg Kinnear mentioned you stopped by that morning. Was she looking to upgrade?"

"Not exactly. A day or two before, I had run into her at the ValleyMart back when it was still Bryce Family Grocers. We were making small talk, and she just dropped into the mix that she was thinking about selling and moving back west. It was a two bed, one bath, and even that felt like too much space for just her.

"I followed up with a phone call that afternoon. Her other son, Kelso, I think, was living with her at the time. She thought about maybe letting him take over the house or just putting it up for a quick sale."

"Did she say why she wanted to sell?"

Grier shook her head and settled back into the large easy chair. "She never spelled it out for me. Her entire demeanor, though, it was—how best to put this—she was distracted, almost melancholy. I got the feeling she wanted to make a new start somewhere else. I think she was seeing Grady Foster at the time, so he may or may not have been a part of that new start. From everything I had heard, it sounded like they were getting serious."

Somewhere in the office complex, a phone bleated an alert. The noise brought the woman out of her memories for just a moment. "Don't worry about that; my assistant will get it." She dismissed the distraction with a wave of one hand.

"Where was I? Shona's house. Well, I didn't push her on it, but if I was to be involved, I really needed to know what exactly she was looking for. She said she was just spitballing. She also asked me to keep it under wraps until she was ready to pull the trigger. I checked with a few neighbors and cobbled together some comps—high if she was selling on the market and low if it was going to Kelso."

Elle waited until the narrative came to a logical end. "What about that morning?"

"The day she died? Let's see." The older woman rested both elbows on the armrests of the chair and tented her fingers under her chin. "I had stopped by probably between nine and ten. We were going over her numbers, and she seemed cautious but optimistic about moving to an actual sale. I think that whatever reservations she had had, she had made up her mind." She sighed. "And that was it. A few hours later, the police were in my office asking me about our visit. All these years later, it's still so hard to believe how someone so lovely can be gone like that in an instant."

"I know it gave us all something to think about," Elle added. "Life can be short."

Grier nodded, slapped her knees with both hands, and stood. "I don't want to keep you here all morning, Elle. That's all I can think to tell you. Since then, I've had very little contact with the Mackay family. I see Dan from time to time, usually just some social event or another. Otherwise, we never really cross paths."

Elle stood and shook the woman's hand. She thanked Grier for her time, accepting a third business card with a promise to call when she was ready to buy. She turned as she made her way through the front courtyard, receiving a wave from the older woman as she watched Elle walk past the gate. Elle waved back; Grier smiled and disappeared from view.

She stepped onto the sidewalk, dodging a pair of young mothers speed-walking and pushing oversized strollers. As she turned onto the side street, she felt immediate relief from the crush of pedestrians that was becoming a daily traffic jam across St. Andrews. A few more paces brought her to where her SUV waited under a broad, shady oak tree. The first thing she noticed was the condition of the rear passenger's side tire.

"Damn," she muttered. A few seconds later, she noticed the front passenger side tire. The rims of both wheels rested securely on the bricked pavement. Each sported a long, deep gash in the sidewall, just below the SUV's wheel wells.

"Damn. Damn. Damn," she repeated as she reached for her shoulder bag. Setting the folio down on the hood, she opened the bag beside it and fished out her cell phone. As she finished dialing roadside service, she saw the writing. Someone had scratched a crude message into the black paint of the car's hood:

Duncan did it.

14

Fear is not cowardice. Acting in a wrong and contemptible manner because of our fear is cowardice.

— R. M. Ballantyne

The tow truck driver was checking the portable brake lights on the back of Elle's SUV when her ex-husband shuffled around the corner off Main. Despite their history, Dan represented a calming force in Elle's life, very much the yin to her yang. He shook his head as he approached and pointed at the rear tire.

"Damn, Ellie. Who'd you tick off this time?"

She rolled her eyes and motioned him over to the front of the vehicle. As the tow truck began to winch the SUV onto the flatbed, Elle pointed to the hood. Dan gave out a slow, low whistle.

"I'd like to say that narrows it down a little, but it doesn't," he added.

"I was around the corner talking to Grier Hammond at Sage Palm Properties. We couldn't have been more than twenty or thirty minutes, and I came back to this."

"Where's he taking it?"

"Gordon's Garage. I know we're not keeping score, but I do owe you one for this."

"Ellie, don't worry about it," he replied with a casual shrug. "As far as the office is concerned, I'm taking a long lunch. I'll drop you at the garage, and you can call me if you need a ride to Lana's place. I'm parked right around the corner."

They rode for a few minutes in silence as Dan navigated the downtown streets. To Elle, he looked tired and out of focus. His eyes suggested a lack of sleep, and his voice hinted at a sore throat or perhaps a night of crying.

"Again, I know we're not keeping score, but Elle, I have to ask you a favor."

She shrugged and shook her head. "You know I can't say yes until I know what it is."

"Yeah, so you're saying that it probably won't be a 'yes' even then." He took a deep breath and exhaled slowly. "I need you to drop all this crap with Duncan Scott and my mother. Jonah Tanner called me yesterday with more questions. He brought it up. He's heard it from a dozen people all over town. This morning, I've heard it firsthand from all those same people. The book, the project, the TV show, whatever it is, I need you to stop."

"Dan," Elle began calmly, "I understand where you're coming from—"

He huffed and stared at her disbelief. "Do you, Ellie?"

"Believe it or not, I do." She held her palms up, attempting to placate him. "I'll give you an answer, but before I do, I've got two questions for you."

He shifted impatiently and answered with a sigh. "Shoot."

Elle tried to keep her tone gentle but serious. "Did you kill Duncan?"

He turned to look her square in the eyes. "Elle, you know I didn't."

"I know you didn't. And did you do that to my car?"

"You expecting me to say, 'Guilty as charged'? Of course, I didn't."

"I know you didn't do that either." She turned in her seat and sought eye contact, willing him to consider her point. "Someone else did. I might be flailing around in the dark, but the one thing I'm sure of now is that someone somewhere out there is worried. I don't know who, and I don't know why, but they are thinking I'm looking under the right rocks."

Dan pulled the car off the street and put it in park. He gripped the steering wheel with both hands and dropped his head. After a few moments, he turned off the engine.

"Ellie, this is…was…part of our problem. You've got this built-in instinct to go against the grain. Everybody else says stop, you say go. They say right, you say left. You're blessed with this independent, wicked smart brain; it's like an engine that's always revving. In fact, it's one of the things I love most about you. But for all that drive and all that horsepower, you don't know how to put on the brakes. For some of us, it's a damn scary ride."

"I'm not doing this just to be right. Honestly, I'm scared for you. First, it was Shona, then Duncan. Even if Duncan was guilty, there's still someone else out there with bad things on their mind. They were willing to kill him with your fork. Somehow, they are tied into this with you and Paige and everyone else. And now this person—well I'm assuming it's the same person—wants to scare me off." She stopped for a moment to let her words sink in then changed her tactic.

"You were telling me maybe two nights ago that you're only thinking about Paige. Me, too, Dan. You're the best, most important thing in her life, and I won't risk any chance that something could happen to you."

"Ellie, I get that, and I know where your heart is. But right now, I can't do this. It's hurting me, and it's really setting Kelsey off. Despite knowing that he killed my mother, I'm actually sorry Duncan's dead; I really am. In the long run, though, I can't help but think that someone did us all a favor. We just want to move on and never think about Duncan again. I can't do that with you playing junior detective. It's not fair to me, and it's not fair to our family."

They sat together in silence without making eye contact. Dan shook his head and turned the key in the ignition, bringing his hand to the gear shift.

"Damn it, Dan," Elle said through a tight jaw. "I'm not saying I have to be right; I'm just saying I might be right. On the slim chance that I am, are you willing to risk that? To just let some person who wants to frame you for murder walk free to try again? What if they succeed? What would that mean for Paige?"

He dropped his hands to his lap, leaving the car idling in neutral. "You come up with these ideas. You pull the pin and toss them in the middle of the room like a hand grenade. When it finally goes off, there's going to be collateral damage."

Elle reached for the passenger armrest and unlocked the car doors.

"Come on, Elle," Dan said in a conciliatory tone. He turned to look at her again, and his shoulders drooped as he relaxed. "Listen, I'm trying to be open and honest with you. I'm not trying to piss you off."

"I *am* pissed off. I'm pissed off at you. I'm pissed off at me. I'm pissed off at my car. See a trend here?" Elle opened the passenger door and undid her seatbelt. Retrieving her bag from the floorboard, she stepped out of the parked car. "I appreciate the ride, Dan. I really do. It's only five or six more blocks. I could use the exercise."

"Elle, I'm sorry," he replied. She closed the door, and he rolled down the window. "This wasn't what I had in mind. I have no problem taking you the rest of the way. We're both bigger than this."

She leaned to the window, kissed her finger, then tagged his cheek with it. "Some days we are, some days we aren't." She took a deep breath and exhaled. "Thanks for being honest about everything. I'm going to walk it off, do a little thinking."

"That sounds like a good idea. Text me when you get home. I'm not convinced you're on the right path with all this, but I do worry about you."

"I worry about you, too." She stepped back from the car and began her walk to Gordon's Garage.

Two blocks later, as she approached the intersection of Main and Elmhurst on foot, Elle was startled by a brief siren and a stream of colored lights. She jumped, nearly dropping her bag. Behind her, an unmarked police cruiser with darkly tinted windows idled, its hidden reds and blues flashing just beneath the grille.

"What the actual hell?" Elle exclaimed, louder than she intended, spreading her open hands as she looked at the cruiser in disbelief.

The car inched forward as the passenger window slid down. Elle marched toward the sedan and glared into the open window. "I'm not even jaywalking here. What is your problem?"

Jonah Tanner gave a sheepish smile from the driver's seat. "I am so sorry, Elle. I completely meant that as a joke. I saw you walking up ahead and just thought I'd give you a jump."

"Jump, massive heart attack, same thing." She turned away from the window, taking a deep breath to head off the adrenaline now running through her.

"Are you OK?" he asked. "You look like you've had a day."

Elle shook her head. "Give me a lift to Gordon's, and I'll think about maybe, someday forgiving you."

Jonah gave an exclamation under his breath and handed Elle her phone. "Whoever it was, they did a number on your car. You sure you don't want to file a police report? You will need to for filing anything with your insurance."

She shook her head and took another look at the words carved into her SUV. "No, I needed new tires, and Gordon will repaint the hood. Roadside assistance covered the tow. Plus, after the damage I did to my truck and Tammy Murray's hatchback, my rates are high enough as it is."

"I really can't argue with that," he admitted.

"How are things going on your end?"

He smiled. "Personally or professionally?" Elle gave him a dry look. "OK, professionally I'm running out of ideas on Duncan Scott. There just isn't anything to go off. The ME confirms the cause of death was the pitchfork. Yes, it was obvious. No, I don't need a sarcastic thank you for that one." Elle gave him a second dry look.

"So, where does that leave us?" he asked as began to count off on his fingers. "One, there's really zero physical evidence other than the weapon. Two, the weapon has no usable trace or fingerprints. Three, literally hundreds of people had unfettered, unobserved access to the scene. Four, there are no eyewitnesses to tie any of these people to the crime or the scene."

"You ran out of fingers at just the right time," Elle remarked.

"And I'm running out of time. Elle, this is going to stay between you and me, but I'm not getting a lot of pressure to close this one out. I know Red MacFarlane has his kilt in a bunch over the murder, but the people signing my time sheet every week don't want much more effort thrown at this one. It doesn't look like an easy win, and frankly, Hopkirk is about ready to chalk it up to an unsolvable revenge killing of a guy who probably deserved it."

"That leaves one big problem," Elle replied. "You know how this town operates. Dan's going to spend the rest of his life as the guy who probably forked Duncan Scott. It's closure for Hopkirk and the town, but not for the Mackays."

As Jonah pulled the unmarked cruiser into an empty garage bay, a large, husky man with gray hair and a deep, weathered tan greeted them. He wiped his fingers on his oil-streaked pant legs before offering them both a handshake. "Miss Elle! Got your car in back. Hey there, Jonah."

"Gordon."

"Well, I took a look at your vehicle," as he spoke his rugged face took on a deadly serious look. "In my professional opinion, it was deliberate."

"So, the two slashed tires and the poorly handwritten message weren't an accident?" Elle asked with a touch of sarcasm.

The mechanic paused for a second then gave a sheepish smile. "Sorry, I didn't realize this was a police thing, so I was trying to keep it all official."

"I'm just along for the ride," Jonah replied. "Wrong place, wrong time."

"Well, in that case, Elle, they cut your tires up real good. Took most of the topcoat off your hood with what was probably just a rock. I can have you back on the road in the morning once the tires come in. I'll buff out the worst of the scratches. If you want, I can set you up with a day next week, and my guy will get it painted for you."

"You're the best," Elle replied. "Call me when it's ready."

"You need a ride, Miss Elle? Keith can take you home."

"I got her," Jonah offered. "Needed to talk to her anyway."

As he slipped into the cruiser, the detective added, "Do me a favor and check her brake lines."

15

The mark of a Scot of all classes is that he remembers and cherishes his forebears, good or bad; and there burns alive in him a sense of identity with the dead even to the twentieth generation.

— Robert Louis Stevenson

Jonah Tanner tapped his fingers to the rhythm of Martha Davis softly singing *Only the Lonely* through the police cruiser's unexceptional sound system. He stole a look at his passenger and turned off the music.

"Elle, I'm worried about you."

"Why?" She looked up from her phone in concern.

"We've been in the car for fifteen minutes. I'm a captive audience here, and you haven't asked me anything else about Duncan Scott."

She sighed and dropped the phone in her lap. "OK, Detective Tanner. Have you learned anything else about the murder of Duncan Scott?"

"I am so glad you asked." He ran his fingers through his hair and gave her a sly smile. "Nope, not a thing."

She laughed. "Is that the only question I get?"

"Of course not; I was just surprised you hadn't brought it up again. Of course, it sounds like you're getting most of your inside scoop from Trey Howard at the moment."

"Word travels fast."

"You have no idea. Around St. Andrews, the police are the last ones to know. Somebody so much as tears the tag off a mattress, and the local network has all the gory details before we've even had our morning coffee. If I play my cards right, I don't even have to leave my desk most days. I can make two or three calls to the right busybodies, and I've got all I need for an arrest warrant without standing up."

"So, what's different about this one?" Elle asked.

"Two things," he replied. "First, it's only been four days. It takes a little time to pull a murder charge together. And second, you're still working on it. I don't want to rush you."

She shrugged and leaned against the tinted passenger window. "I'm dragging my feet because we haven't discussed my fee yet."

"Elle, have you seen our budget? Unless your fee is a gift card from Burger Castle, you're out of our league."

"You can put it on my tab. So, if I get another question…"

"Shoot."

"What are you thinking about Dan?"

"Dan? Well, women seem to find him attractive. Good build. Doting father. Snappy dresser. Questionable taste in women. Or is it a taste for questionable women?"

She laughed out loud; it felt good. Jonah had a knack for defusing difficult situations, a talent, she imagined, that made him one hell of a police interviewer. "Smart ass."

"No, in all seriousness, I think you can rest easy; Dan is off the hook. My only suspect is in the clear, and that's the biggest reason I'm not making much progress."

"What put him in the clear?" Elle asked with a hint of anticipation.

"We don't have anyone who can place him for most of the early afternoon. However, several people saw him before and during lunch. By that point, two of the other athletes remember Dan's fork missing for at least an hour or two. It wouldn't make sense for him to hide the weapon in a fit of rage, nap and have lunch, then retrieve the weapon to off Duncan."

"Is that your way of saying I was right?"

"Six of one, half a dozen of another."

"What do you think about Duncan and Shona?"

Jonah shook his head and drummed his fingers on the steering wheel.

"OK, I got your email about that. Actually, I got all seven of your emails about that and the two texts. I get your points about the cord, the handprint, and the guest room. They don't seem to make sense, but I have to tell you that when it comes to murder, people don't always make sense.

"Most of us have no experience killing another human being. It's messy and brutal and incredibly difficult, both during and after the crime. People don't follow their routines when it comes to something like this. Yes, most of us may be predictable most days, but this isn't most days. It's likely the worst day any of us will ever experience."

"You don't see any merit to what I'm suggesting?"

He shook his head and furrowed his brow a bit. "I'm not saying that. In fact, you bring up some damn good points. The bigger problem is that this is a non-starter. The original victim is long dead; the accused and convicted killer is also dead. The family isn't hounding us for an update. My higher-ups are looking the other way. The DA is fine where things stand. No matter how on target your observations are, you are the only one still knocking around on this one."

Elle fiddled with the glovebox latch as she reconsidered her approach. "Are you telling me to drop it?" Elle asked.

"I'm not naïve enough to think you would. You're going to do your thing; we both know that. So, I'm not telling, I'm asking. I'm asking you to do exactly what you want to do, but please, Elle, be smart and be careful. This car thing wasn't much, but you've pissed off somebody."

Elle gave a quick smile of victory. "That's my point, Jonah. I've pissed somebody off. That somebody has done something they are willing to take risks to cover up." She paused to let her words sink in. "We know you have still have Duncan's murder on the table. You and I both know you there's a chance you might still have Shona's murder on the same table."

Jonah crossed his arms across the steering wheel and slumped forward slightly in his seat. "I see where you're going with this."

Elle nodded. "Best case? You've got plenty of time to find Duncan's murderer and wrap this up. You get a nice plaque, the newspapers get a delicious story, and the higher ups get to go back to bigger and better things."

She paused again for effect. "Worst case? Someone else murdered Shona. That means you've got two dead bodies with the killer—or killers—still walking among us in our community. Even worse, in my eyes, at least, an innocent young man spent five years in jail only to end up murdered himself. I know you, Jonah. In your heart, you know what happened to Duncan Scott may not be right. That's not justice. And I plan to make damn sure that all these questions get answers."

The detective brought the car to a slow stop and leaned back in his seat with an audible exhale. "I thought you'd say something like that."

Without a car, Elle felt restless. After Jonah dropped her off on Douglas Drive, she popped into her mother's house only long enough to drop her bag and leash Angus. They both, she felt, needed a good walk in the late afternoon sun. Over the next half hour, she strolled the oak-lined streets of the old St. Andrews neighborhoods, passing Campbell Avenue, Stewart Street, Docherty Avenue, and a dozen others. From her early years, Elle remembered each of these names as simply another place on which a friend or teacher may live. They remained an integral part of her childhood memories.

Although her mother was a more recent immigrant from Scotland, Elle had spent her adult years studying the waves of Caledonians who populated what is modern-day North Carolina. Many of the families and friends she had come to know were originally part of a mass influx of their countrymen over four hundred years ago. In the 1600s, these first Scots arrived in the region, bringing with them the Gaelic language and traditions of their homeland.

In 1739, one group of immigrants founded the Argyll Colony, the first fully Scottish community in the region. Although the assembly first wintered near Newton—now known as Wilmington—they eventually settled further down the Cape Fear River at Cross Creek outside of Fayetteville. Over the next few decades, a steady wave of immigrations brought more than 20,000 of these settlers to the Carolina coastal region. By the late 1770s, the area was known to many as the Valley of the Scots, owing to the booming population of Highland transplants.

Closer to home, Elle recognized that the names of these streets and the people who once bore them were an important part of her town's history. As she turned the corner from Campbell onto Clark, she recalled two early town founders—Edmund Campbell and Genevieve, originally *Genovefa*, Clark. In another block, she knew she'd cross Mackenzie Way, named for the colonial-era merchant brothers Amiel and Israel Mackenzie. Their warehouses once lined the eastern end of Eagle Island, only recently replaced with fashionable lofts and a packed dining promenade.

As she and Angus rounded the block, they passed a few streets named for the later settlers, including Mahala Sutherland, August Docherty, and Gideon MacUspaig. Mahala operated one of the first woman-owned businesses on the island. Her boarding house offered comfortable accommodations for grounded sea travelers and itinerant workers. August owned much of the farmland that once surrounded the northern parts of St. Andrews. As for the members of Clan MacUspaig, Elle was all too familiar with how their stories ended.

Most of these families had long since left the island, but their names and their histories remained. Their past influenced and guided the present, even as new bloodlines took their place among the town's elder statespeople.

On cue, Elle passed a *For Sale* sign, and Grier Hammond's smiling face promised service that was both dependable and extraordinary. It was a face that blended the best qualities of age, congeniality, and shrewd business acumen. Vee and the realtor were cut from the same cloth. Elle could picture her mother and Grier being the staunchest of rivals, the best of friends, or likely both.

As she steered the basset hound off Basalt Avenue and back onto Douglas Drive, her phone buzzed with an incoming text. "Don't know where you wandered off to, but Mama says dinner is ready. Also, Angus is missing."

"On our way in 5," Elle replied, adding a dog emoji.

"Help me put away the whites, and I'll give you a ride back to Lana's." Vee patted the dining room chair next to her. On the table sat stacks of unfolded napkins, washcloths, and placemats. The room smelled of warm linen with a faint hint of bleach.

"How do you go through so many of these each week?" Elle asked, setting down her leather folio and picking up a pair of pristine cotton glass towels. She sat and started folding.

"With the twins eating over so often, the laundry does pile up quickly. But placemats and cloth napkins are important; it's never too early to teach them proper manners." Vee continued to fold as her eyes shifted to her daughter. "Now, I don't want to pry, but Paige said Dan and you had a few words."

"It's nothing, Mama. He wants me to walk away from whatever's going on with Duncan and his mother."

"What does your heart tell you?"

"It tells me..." She thought for a moment. "It tells me that I'm on the right track. At the same time, another voice is saying that I should just leave it alone. It's in the past at this point, and Jonah will do what the police need to do."

Vee stacked the finished napkins and folded her hands over them in contemplation. "Ellie, that isn't the woman I raised. I meant what I said to Paige the other day. The wheels of justice are often swift enough, but sometimes, they need a little push.

"I believe that God watches everything we do. He also has a lot on his plate, with all the hurricanes and floods and professional athletes and award-winners to look after. It never hurts to give him a second set of eyes and a few extra hands. With you doing what you do best, the guilty can't hide forever, and the truth will be revealed."

Elle felt a flood of recognition and relief. Perhaps, she thought, she truly was on the right path. "Thanks, Mama."

"More importantly, I agree with you. I think Duncan Scott was innocent."

Her hands stopped, mid-fold. "You do?"

"I do, but that leaves us with more questions than answers. If not Duncan, then who?"

"I haven't figured out that part, Mama. St. Andrews is a small town, but everyone is so interconnected. It's like a web that you can't get out of."

"So, give me your best ideas. Who had easiest access to Shona?"

"Maybe it's something to do with Grady Foster? A lover's quarrel? Or he got upset because she was leaving town without him. He's in good shape for an elderly fellow, and this was more than five years ago."

Vee scoffed at the remark. "Elderly? Ellie, he's two years younger than I am. And I don't believe that Grady would kill any more than you do. Despite his advanced age and swiftly approaching death, he doesn't strike me as the violent type. And why frame poor Duncan?"

"That's the odd thing," Elle replied. "When Duncan got locked up, Grady was his only visitor. Several times, in fact."

"I don't want to think ill of someone like Grady, but perhaps he was feeling guilty? That would explain the visits. Perhaps it was Grady and not Dan that Duncan had come to the park to see."

"That thought crossed my mind, Mama. If we're looking purely at temper, Kelsey Mackay has the shortest fuse."

Vee wrinkled her nose and gave her head a quick shake. "I don't think even you would seriously consider that."

"You're right. I've always heard that Dan was a devoted son, but Kelsey was the mama's boy. There's no way he could do that to her."

"Orna or Grier?"

"I can't imagine either one of them coming up with something like this. Peg, too. And none of them had anything to gain from her death. And in Grier's case, she probably lost a quick sale."

Vee pursed her lips and let her eyes drift off into the distance. With a quick smile, she piled and straightened the last of the placemats. She took the stack and placed them carefully in a hutch drawer next to the playing cards. "Let's go back to the beginning. Let's start with Shona."

"What else is there to uncover about her?"

"Well, how about I tell you what I know about the Mackays." Vee retook the chair next to Elle and cornered the tablecloth. She waited a moment, fixing Elle with a sharp, expectant stare. "Aren't you going to write this down?" She reached across her daughter and tapped the leather folio with one finger.

"You talk, I'll decide what I need to remember."

"Suit yourself. I knew Shona Mackay socially before you and Dan made your...connection. She shared an office not far from All in a Row. She and two other women used the space for their bookkeeping or accounting businesses or whatever. I think one of Shona's partners still has the office.

"Over the years, she probably worked for everyone at one point or another. She worked for Kirk, obviously, the Salted Jack before Buster took over, the marina, Grady when he was with the chamber, the Bryce family, McLeane Spirits, Highlands Construction, and may have worked for Coira at one time. I think Stuart even hired her for the Roan Games based on a recommendation from Red Macfarlane. Of course, that was before Caroline married into the family."

"I didn't know Shona was connected to Red and the old Roan Island Games."

"In a town like this, everyone has worked for everyone else. In fact, did you know that Orna Gunn was one of my first hires at All in a Row?"

Elle was genuinely shocked. "She didn't mention it. She mentioned just about everything else she could think of, but not that. She didn't remember ever meeting me before."

"Hogwash," her mother replied with a smirk. "She's met you a dozen times to Sunday. That woman has no memory for anything that doesn't titillate her baser sensibilities. That's why I had to eventually let her go. She was a hard worker and a whirlwind on windows, but also an irascible gossip. I couldn't trust her discretion. In my work, we have so much access to people's personal lives, their hidden secrets. We have to know when to speak and when to hold our tongues."

"Did Shona ever work for you?"

"Of course not, Ellie. I've always done my own books. I'm not about to let my business live and die by someone else's misplaced decimal point. You're still not writing any of this down."

She sighed and looked around the room, deciding the comment wasn't worth a response. All the laundry was folded, leaving her little to do with her hands, so she fiddled with her pencil as she glanced at the notes in her folio. "So, Mama, do you think her work had anything to do with her death?"

"I can't think of any other reason someone would want her gone. When you play with numbers, it's always a short-range game. Sooner or later, a bill won't get paid, or a late notice will slip through. A smart businessperson will figure it out."

"Maybe there was something up at the bar?"

"Could be, but is it worth killing for, really? Let's say Kirk or Peg caught Shona with her hand in the till. Killing her wouldn't bring the money back. They'd be better off exposing her and pursuing a civil case. Did Peg mention anything about Kirk when you spoke to her?"

"Just that Shona did their books," Elle replied. "They went under not long after, but officially, that was due to the fire and Kirk's death. Still, it might be something I try to pin down with Peg. She was happy to talk the first time; maybe I should give her another try."

"How about this? Why not check with Effie McLeane, too? She's a smart one, and she's been in business as long as I have. I can give her a call for you tonight. Why not ask her if she ever had any concerns about Shona's work?"

"Mama, that would be amazing. I'm free any time she is." She relaxed back in her chair and took an easy breath, relieved to have the next step in sight.

"In the meantime, Ellie, I've got a few ideas of my own."

16

Today's rain is tomorrow's whisky.

— Scottish Proverb

The thunderstorm started early on Thursday morning. As Elle looked out the kitchen window, she regretted her choice of walking to Gordon's Garage. She rinsed her empty coffee mug and watched the rain beat against the glass panes.

"Great day to be alive," Lana said as she gave her sister a hug from behind. She was dressed in a white silk blouse, blue linen blazer, flannel pajama bottoms, and fuzzy bedroom slippers. She dumped the last contents of her cereal bowl in the sink and set it to one side of the counter. "What's up with you this morning?"

She gave Lana's wardrobe choices a critical eye. "Well, I was going to ask you for a ride to pick up my car, but from what I'm seeing, you probably shouldn't be driving."

"I've got a video call in ten. It's a new client who needs some basic contract work. It'll be dull as dirt, but it pays hourly plus a retainer. Later, I've got dinner scheduled with Red and some of the others on a board structure for the new games. Plus, I think Mama already took care of you."

"What do you mean?" Elle asked. As she spoke, the doorbell rang.

"That must be your ride," Lana replied. She grabbed an apple from a basket on the island and disappeared into her office.

Dan stood at the front door, wet umbrella in hand. His beard had been trimmed, and his eyes looked bright and focused. For the first time since Saturday morning, Elle felt he looked like his old self again.

"Vee said you'd be needing a ride," he said, gesturing to the Subaru idling in the morning rain.

Despite their disagreement the day before, Elle felt her spirits rise. "She was righter than she knew."

"You're up and around earlier than I'm used to. I figured I'd be here half an hour early. This is a new side of you."

"Yeah, I'm just full of surprises. Hungry, too. Do you have time for a quick breakfast?"

From their corner booth at Top o' the Morning, Elle and Dan made small talk over scrambled eggs and buckwheat pancakes. She added another pat of butter to the stack before realizing she had poured far too much blueberry syrup.

"You know, you don't have to buy me breakfast. The ride was on the house," Dan said. His eyes dropped to her plate. "And if you want to trade pancakes, I never get too much syrup."

"I need to learn to live with my own mistakes," Elle replied as she used her knife to squeegee some of the liquid off her pancakes. While most stayed on the plate, a river of blue dripped off the table and onto her pants leg. "Damn. And I wanted to talk. I figured that there's an audience here, so we'll be on our best behavior."

He handed her a napkin. "Never stopped us before."

"True."

Dan took another bite of eggs, then set his fork down. He gave Elle a thoughtful look. "How about I begin?" He took a deep breath. "Listen, I, in no way, meant to come for you yesterday. So, I want to apologize."

Elle waved it off with a warm smile. "No apology needed."

"No, I know you, and I know where this is coming from. I just have Kelsey yapping in one ear, and my own fears and worries barking in the other. I'm not at my best this week, and I don't want to take it out on you."

She looked him square in the eye. "Thank you, Dan. I promise you, I'm not trying to be right. I'm just thinking about you and Paige. That's it, honest."

He gave a low chuckle. "So, I'm just thinking about you, and you're just thinking about me. This doesn't sound right."

"If we are both so selfless and thoughtful, where did we go wrong?" As she spoke, her phone began to vibrate. She picked it up and dropped it in her open purse.

Dan took a moment to chew a slice of bacon. "This was my second time getting married, and I thought I had all the kinks worked out from the first go-round. God knows, that was a disaster. I haven't even seen or spoken to Becky in twelve years."

"I still can't believe you married a Becky," Elle added with a smirk.

"It's about the same time you were shacking up with a Chad."

"So, that's one point for each of us. You and Paige have still never heard anything from her?"

"Nope. Her sister sends Paige a card every year on her birthday. Last we heard, Becky is still overseas, 'finding her true path' or whatever it's called now. But as I was saying, my first marriage was a disaster. You and I wasted no time making it official, but I thought we really had a chance."

"So did I," Elle replied between bites of pancake. She met his eyes and recalled those early days of hope and excitement as they planned a future together. It may not have been meant to be, but they had tried their best.

"When we didn't work out, I felt like I had failed as a husband. Worse, I knew I was failing as a father. I don't want Paige thinking that this is how marriage should be." From Elle's purse, the phone began to vibrate again.

"You're still one up on me, Dan. This is my one and only, and all I have to show for it is a few misdemeanor charges that will disappear in a year or two." She held up a pair of crossed fingers for emphasis. "At least you got Paige for all your heartache. My big worry now is that I'm just not marriage material."

Dan shook his head. "I disagree with you on that one. Don't get me wrong. I think you will always do just fine on your own. You're even better, though, when you've got someone watching your back. Then you can just jump into life headfirst and do your thing the best way you know how."

Elle wasn't sure if it was the conversation, the morning sun through the restaurant windows, or the plate full of pancakes, but she felt truly happy. "Seriously, Dan. Where is all this warm, fuzzy goodwill coming from?"

He laughed and shrugged. "Don't hate him even more than you already do, but I've been listening to Kelsey trash you for the past three days. It's just nonstop. I had to defend you, so I just told him to shut it down. Standing up for you reminded me of all the things I admire about you."

An electronic chime sounded from Elle's purse. She sighed and set aside her fork and knife.

"Come on, I'm trying to have a moment here." She opened her purse and grabbed the phone before the reminder could chime. As she flipped through her notifications, she found herself reading it a second, then third time. Once it finally registered, her mouth fell open. "Oh, God."

The rain began to slow and fade as Dan pulled onto Selkirk Drive. An ambulance and three police cars blocked access to the Mackay house and its neighbors on either side. Overhead, a news helicopter from a Wilmington affiliate hovered amongst the parting rainclouds. A small group of curiosity seekers whispered and shook their umbrellas in Orna Gunn's front yard. Yellow tape kept them off the sidewalk and away from the bustling emergency workers.

Dan pulled along the curb two houses down, and they both walked toward his family home. As the pair approached the Mackay front yard, they were intercepted by Kelsey. His long hair was disheveled, and his bloodshot eyes indicated he had been crying. Dan took a step around Elle, putting himself directly in his younger brother's path.

"Move, Dan," Kelsey growled. "You can hide on the sidelines if you want, but this is between me and her." He jabbed a finger in Elle's direction, his eyes locked onto hers with a barely contained rage. "Everything here is her fault. Not Mom's, not mine, not even that bastard Duncan's. Hers."

Dan stood tall, matching the bigger man's attempts to sidestep him, and keeping himself a protective barrier between the pair. He put his face in front of his brother's and spoke with a firm warning. "Kelsey, back it up."

"To hell with you, Dan. Mom's dead, the guy who killed her got his, and she just won't let it go. He got exactly what he deserved. Nothing she's going to say or do will change that." He glared over Dan's shoulder to Elle and snarled, "Stay the hell away from me. I swear to God, I'll end this myself."

From Peg Kinnear's yard, Jonah Tanner spoke up. "I'm going to pretend I didn't hear that, Mackay. You've had a rough day. Why don't you take it back inside and cool off for a bit."

Kelsey looked from the detective to Elle and back again. He shook his head and spat on the ground. "This isn't over," he whispered to Elle with a growl. Without making eye contact with his older brother, he turned and went back inside the family home.

As the front door slammed, Grady Foster approached Dan and Elle from across the street. "I just heard." The older man looked pale and distracted. He shook his head as he watched the emergency personnel at work.

Elle reached out and took his hand. "Us, too. We just got here."

"I'm going to go check on Kelsey. Please fill me in when you can."

"Why don't you take him for a ride? Maybe get him something to eat or drink?" Dan suggested.

Grady nodded and gave Dan's shoulder a squeeze. He knocked on the Mackays' front door. After a few moments, the door opened, and he disappeared inside.

As Jonah waved the pair over, Elle and Dan slipped under the yellow tape and crossed the Kinnear front yard. "I know neither of you have any official business here, but I wanted to talk to you before this got over town."

"If Grady is here, it sounds like it's already lighting up the network," Elle replied.

"On the surface, this looks like Peg had a cut-and-dry accident," Jonah continued, "but my instincts are telling me this is another quagmire that's opening up."

"Can you tell us what happened?" Dan asked.

"I'll give you some details, but please don't repeat these. Orna Gunn found Peg Kinnear about thirty minutes ago. She had come over to borrow... I don't know, it was flour or sugar or something... And she found Peg at the bottom of the basement stairs. It looks like she had been carrying a box up from the lower level, missed a step at the top, and took a bad tumble all the way down. She must have hit the ground hard. I doubt she ever regained consciousness, and she bled out on the basement floor."

Elle felt a rush of blood in her ears. The confrontation with Kelsey had her adrenaline pumping, and the confirmation of Peg's death made her head spin.

"The EMTs couldn't do anything for her," Jonah continued. "I've got Jeannie and Glen checking the house for anything suspicious or out of place. Normally, we wouldn't give an accident like this a second thought, but right now, we can't be too careful. I'm going way beyond just checking the boxes on this one."

As he finished, Officer Glen Lewis escorted Orna from around the corner of the house to the young detective. She was wearing a different kaftan, this one festooned with Asian-inspired birds and flowers. On both arms, a series of colorful plastic bangles clicked as she talked.

"Detective Tanner," she called, nearly at a run, waving and rattling both arms. Elle resisted the urge to leap from the woman's trajectory. "Elle, Daniel, it's been simply awful. I can't begin to describe what I've been through." She stopped just short of plowing Elle over.

From the front porch, Glen called out, "I've taken her statement. She's all yours, Detective." His mission complete, he ducked back into the Kinnear house.

"Miss Gunn, I'm sorry for your loss," Jonah began. He held his hands up, as if trying to calm a wild animal. When she stilled a bit, he continued in an apologetic tone. "I know you've told Officer Lewis what happened, but I'd appreciate your version while it's still fresh in your memory, if you don't mind."

"Of course, Detective. Now?" The woman gave Elle and Daniel a sideways glance.

"It's OK, Miss Gunn. Elle's research has been a valuable part of our recent investigations."

"You can never be too careful," she replied. "Everyone always listening in and just *aching* to spread bad news without a thought to the consequences. As I told your colleague, I had come over right at 9:42, give or take a minute, to borrow a cup of elderberry preserves. I've had the most awful sore throat, and elderberry is the one sure cure for hoarseness. Simply boil two tablespoons with a pint of water and add—"

"This was at 9:42?" Jonah interjected.

"Oh, yes, give or take a minute. Peg's car was in the drive, and I knew she'd be home. I hadn't seen anyone come or go, so I had no worries about disturbing her with a guest. I knocked a few times but got no answer. I finally let myself in. It's the kind of thing we neighbors do when we've been here so long. We're practically family. I called out to no answer, so I went toward the kitchen.

"As I passed the door to the basement, I noticed it was slightly ajar. I opened it..." She paused to take a deep breath. "Poor Peg was lying at the bottom of the stairs. Even from the hall, I could tell she wasn't breathing, and with all that blood everywhere, what could one possibly do?"

"Did you check for a pulse?" Elle asked.

"Gracious, no! I could see that she was dead, and I certainly wasn't going down there. Those stairs had killed once today. I wasn't going to give them the satisfaction of a second victim." The woman nodded her head in triumph.

"What *did* you do?" Jonah asked.

"What anyone else would do," she replied. "I called 911. Then I called my good friends Evelyn, Diedre, and Enora. For emotional support, of course."

"Did you notice anything else you think might be worth mentioning?"

"Nothing at all, Detective."

"Well, I thank you for your help. I must ask you to please not discuss this with anyone, particularly the details, until we've completed our investigation."

Orna held up three fingers as a formal oath. "Of course, Detective. I understand how important discretion is in a trying time like this."

As the older woman made her way to the street, the waiting bystanders greeted her with a buzz of excitement. "It was *dreadful*," she began in a voice that carried across the yard.

Jonah sighed and looked to Dan. "Would you mind keeping an eye on her? She's going to talk, a lot, but I want to know if she adds anything she left out before. I'm going to talk to Elle for a minute."

"I'll leave you two to it," Dan replied as he darted after Jonah's prime witness.

17

Kindness and courage can repair time's faults.

— Edwin Muir

In the Kinnear garage, Elle flipped through a series of photos on Jonah Tanner's cell phone. "This is as close as I can let you get to the basement," he said. "Even this could get me in trouble." As he spoke, he gave a knowing look to the pair of attending officers. Elle had met both more than once, sometimes socially, but more often, in their line of work.

"Didn't see a thing," Glen Lewis replied as he played Cookie Crush on his cell phone.

"Me neither," Jeannie Pace added, "particularly if I can get that Friday time off approved for the Panthers game." Jonah made a quick note in his spiral pad.

In each photo, Peg Kinnear lay on the concrete floor, her body brightly lit by a single light source—a naked ceiling bulb, Elle guessed. Her thin frame was clothed in the same sort of cleaning outfit Elle had seen a few days prior. A large carboard box of books, old encyclopedias from the looks of them, lay to her left, turned over on its side. A dark red pool of blood connected her body and the books as it spread toward the drain in the center of the floor.

"Those steps really did a number on her," Elle commented, noting the fresh bruising on her neck and arms and the pair of clearly evident wounds to the side of her head.

"She took one hell of a fall," Jonah replied, "but there was far more blood than I'd expect, even for a woman of her age and in her condition. From what we could find in her medicine cabinet, she was on apixaban, which is a strong blood thinner. That plus the weight of those encyclopedias certainly didn't help. Earliest guess is that she's been dead for less than an hour. I'll know more when the ME has a chance to look her over. Until then, I'm treating it as an accident. A suspicious one, but still just an accident."

"Why did you need me out here for this?" Elle asked, handing the detective back his phone.

"Really, just two questions," he replied.

"Well, I can answer one right away. Dan has been with me all morning."

Jonah furrowed his brow. "Like, all morning or all night *and* morning?"

Elle shook her head. "That's nobody's business but my own."

"You go, girl," Jeannie added and offered Elle an open-handed high five.

"Actually, though, it was just all morning," she admitted. "We were finishing up breakfast at Top o' the Morning when you called."

"That's certainly good to know," Jonah continued, "but it's not one of the questions. At this point, Dan is completely in the clear, for this and for Duncan Scott. My questions are specifically about you. Have you found out anything else about what happened to your car? With everything this morning, it puts that situation in a completely different light."

Elle gave a quick shrug. "Nothing since you dropped me off at the garage. After breakfast, Dan was giving me a ride to pick up my SUV. Gordon hasn't said anything else to me, though."

"In retrospect, I wish now I had encouraged you to file a police report."

"What good would that have done? Would you all have dusted for fingerprints or canvassed the neighborhood?"

"Probably not," Jonah admitted, "but we would have an official record of the crime. It could help if we are building a case later, and it turns out that your car and Peg Kinnear encountered the same individual."

"Got it. And second?"

"Second, do you have anything else you want to share about Scott or Shona Mackay? At this point, I'm open to any and all screwball theories."

"I'm going to ignore that 'screwball' jab. And no, nothing new to discuss. I'm fleshing out a couple of blanks, and I've got an appointment with Effie McLeane right after lunch. I'll give you a call tomorrow, and we can do a better job of comparing notes."

"I'm going to give you my same warning as always, Elle. Please keep your eyes open. Even when you're on your best behavior, dangerous situations seem to find you. Stay safe for me."

"Will do, Jonah." As she turned to leave the garage, Elle noticed Kelsey Mackay and Grady Foster walking toward the older man's car. She paused mid-step.

Turning back to the detective, she asked, "One quick favor? Can I use a sink inside to wash my hands? My fingers got covered in blueberry syrup at breakfast. And yes, I promise to stay away from the basement."

Standing at the sink in Peg Kinnear's kitchen, Elle took her time washing and rewashing her hands with dish soap. The room was quiet, with a patter of voices coming from the hallway and open front door. In the center of the kitchen table, a slice of orange cake lay on a plate next to the glass-covered stand.

"I can't believe how sticky this syrup is," she said aloud to no one in particular. After a few minutes, Jeannie Pace, her police chaperone, was called away. Elle quickly dried her hands and stepped onto the back patio. With no one in sight, she was able to move unseen behind the dwarf magnolia trees parsed out between the Kinnear and Mackay houses. In less than ten seconds, she stood on Kelsey's back patio, looking into the Mackay family den.

From her perch outside, the interior looked dimly lit and dated. Based on the few times she had visited the home, she knew that the house had been virtually untouched since Shona's murder. Kelsey and his one-time girlfriend Molly Blake had moved out briefly following his mother's death. After a week, perhaps two, he had moved back into the master bedroom.

In the intervening years, Dan noted that Kelsey had changed little. The den sofa, a pillowy leather set with excessive wear, still stood against the main wall facing the sliding glass doors. To her right, Elle could just make out a massive pine entertainment cabinet that once held a cathode ray television, DVD player, and VCR.

The house apparently empty, Elle gave the sliding door handle a tug. After a second, firmer pull, the panel slid open, providing just enough of a gap to allow her entry. As she poked her head into the empty room, she was hit with a mix of stale air and old cigarette smoke. The carpet crunched beneath her feet as she stepped into the den, pausing for several seconds to listen in silence. She tried to close the door behind her, but it only slid forward a few inches.

"Hello?" she called. After a few more moments with no answer, she stepped further into the room and scanned the meager furnishings. The only furniture that looked newer than the rest were four simple dining room chairs positioned around a small table. The wide wooden surface was pocked with cigarette burns and water stains. In the center sat an arrangement of plastic flowers, grimy under a layer of dust.

As she stood in the center of the den, she pictured Shona Mackay, bound to a chair that had long since been banished from the home. She tried to imagine what she had seen before and during the attack. Her efforts left her depressed.

Moving to her left, Elle crossed to a short hallway past the sofa. Behind a closed door, a single bathroom sported a Formica counter covered in men's toiletries and half-empty cans of beer. Further down the hall, a second closed door revealed a small bedroom. Like the rest of the house, the furniture was dated, but here, each piece felt less worn. Despite air that was warm and viscous, the bed and dressing set looked clean and well cared for. A woman's dressing robe hung on a single wall hook, and the vanity was set with older perfume bottles, cosmetics, and a styling brush.

Elle returned to the hall and closed the door behind her. At the end of the corridor, a larger bedroom was in a more serious state of disarray. A queen-sized bed filled one corner, a stained bedspread covering a jumble of unwashed sheets. Piles of men's jeans and work shirts dotted the floor, and most of the flat surfaces were covered in empty cigarette packs and more beer cans.

The only area that had received any care or attention lay around the mirror on the far wall. Tucked into the mirror's frame were a dozen or so photos and color copies. In each, Kelsey Mackay could be seen smiling on Christmas morning, showing off a catch, riding his bike, and blowing out candles. In a few, Dan Mackay stood behind his brother, grinning and mugging for the photographer.

In several of the pictures, Shona was partially visible, her face usually obscured by a hand or conveniently out of frame. Despite the dim light of the master bedroom, Elle could make out the woman's signature red hair. Unlike Elle's own hair, which she'd term classic ginger at best, Shona's crown of curls reflected a natural copper with highlights of auburn and rose gold.

Elle sighed. She knew she was seeing the final pieces of a broken family. The images were slivers and shards that had been pieced back together into something that could never approximate the original. For the first time, she questioned her intrusion into Kelsey's private world. She began to regret the ease with which she had invaded his most personal space.

As she made her way back down the hallway, an electronic ringtone broke the silence. Somewhere past the den, a phone played "Tequila" by the Champs. Stepping toward the sliding glass door, she froze as she heard the front door open.

"I hear it in here," Grady Foster's voice called from the entry hall. Unsure whether she could squeeze out the half-open door, Elle opted to wedge herself behind the pine entertainment cabinet. The corner space was filled with cobwebs, dust bunnies, and long-forgotten video cassettes. She braced herself against the wall and held her breath.

From behind the flat-screen TV, she could see the older man search the sofa cushions and retrieve a smart phone. "I've got it, Kelsey." The younger Mackay brother walked into view from the dining room and pocketed his phone. He stepped toward the hall, and Elle heard him call out.

"Grady, did you open the bathroom?" Not waiting for an answer, he closed the door behind him with a click.

From the den, Grady seemed to be reiterating a point as he raised his voice over the sound of running water. "I know this has been hard, but you must believe me when I say it's all part of God's plan. He had a plan for you and your mother, and He had a plan for Duncan Scott. God has seen that plan through, as He always will. You simply have to have faith."

As he spoke, he noticed the slightly ajar sliding glass door. He opened the door a bit more and stuck his head out. Seeing nothing, he stepped back, forced the door closed, and switched the lock. After a quiet moment, Elle heard the toilet flush, and Kelsey rejoined the older man in the den.

"I don't have your faith," Kelsey admitted. "Sometimes, I wish I did."

Grady clapped him on the shoulder. "It's officially lunchtime, so let me buy you a beer."

After she heard the front door snap shut, Elle counted to twenty, then ten more to be certain. She slipped from behind the pine cabinet, unlocked the glass door, and stepped on to the back patio. This time, she made sure to close the door behind her.

"Where did you disappear to?" Dan asked as they pulled away from the curb. Veering sharply into a three-point turn, he slowed the car to a stop. A pair of EMTs wheeled a figure on a covered gurney down the Kinnear driveway. After a moment of positioning, the medics loaded the body into the waiting ambulance. The thinning crowd that remained across Selkirk Drive stood in mute reverence.

"I needed to wash my hands, then took a minute to stand out back and take a break from all of this," she replied in only half truth. She watched as the ambulance doors closed, and the familiar pair of officers conferred with the driver. The sight further depressed her while steeling her resolve to uncover whatever truth lay beneath.

"One more thing, Dan," she continued. "When all this is over, take some time and reach out to Kelsey."

He slowed the car and regarded her with a furrowed brow. "You're being awfully magnanimous. I don't think he'll ever be ready to patch things up with you."

"It's not for me. I know he's angry, and he has every right to be. I'd be a volcano if anyone ever hurt Mama. I also think he's hurting on a level even he doesn't see. Just promise you'll check in with him. He could use your love and friendship, whether he realizes it or not."

"I promise, I will."

"Thanks, Dan. If you can drop by Gordon's now, I should be able to get to the meeting with Effie McLeane. Before I forget to ask, did Orna add anything to her account once she had a bigger audience?"

"Nothing of any value. She managed to power through the most shocking parts three or four times. Each time, the pool of blood grew bigger. Deeper, too. She's certain there weren't any cars parked on the street this morning, and she didn't see anyone walking either. Whoever it was either slipped in when she was preoccupied or came in from the woods to the north."

He thought for a moment, then turned to Elle. "Mind if I do a little detective guesswork this time?"

She looked back at him with wide eyes and nodded. "Go for it."

"If this wasn't an accident, then there's one important fact. It's just like what happened to Mom and Duncan. I don't think that Peg put up any resistance. Each of them was taken either completely by surprise, or they knew the person that killed them."

Dan paused as Elle turned away from his observations. They rode for several minutes in silence.

"I know this is difficult to discuss, Dan, but thank you for talking it through with me. I need your perspective on this." He made a sharp left, pulled up along the curb at the garage, and put the car into park. "Let's talk tonight if you're around."

18

He goes long barefoot that waits for dead men's shoes.

— Scottish Proverb

The offices for McLeane Spirits were shoehorned into an old counting house near the revitalized docks district in St. Andrews. On either side of the building, two hastily constructed apartment buildings attempted to blend early American wharf realness with post-modern economy. Enormous signage outlined in period-inappropriate Edison bulbs announced leasing now available at the Shipyard and the Dox.

Elle parked on the brick-paved side street in a space topped with a small sign ("You could be home now!") and walked across the small plaza to her appointment. A worn wooden sign announced McLeane Spirits while a newer, cheaper vinyl sign trumpeted Barley & Barrels Craft Brewery. Elle checked her watch and entered the building.

As the massive bottle glass-set oak door closed behind her, she looked around the office lobby. The front room was finished in heavy, Colonial replica furniture, and the air smelled faintly of hops and yeast. The walls and floors were finished in a somber palette of black paint and dark woods. The high ceilings and wide hallway suggested a space more accustomed to merchant commerce than office workers. She found the workspace oddly quiet for a weekday afternoon with only the hum of distant machinery to break the silence.

"Hello?" she called out. After several moments with no answer, she checked her calendar app to confirm her appointment.

"Two o'clock on the nose," she murmured.

Down the dimly lit central hallway, a lock turned, and a large barn door rolled aside. Effie McLeane emerged from the darkness, a wooden clipboard in one hand and a ballpoint pen in the other. She looked as Elle had always remembered her: short, even for a St. Andrews native, with a solid build and simple style. Her steel gray hair was twisted up in a loose bun with a second pen tucked within for convenience. A large canvas satchel rested on one shoulder.

"I should have put the lights on," Effie said in greeting. "It's been such an odd week; I completely forgot that today was Thursday." She reached out and gave Elle a firm, perfunctory handshake.

"Are you the only one here today?" Elle asked.

"I'm the only one here most days, and I'm done for the afternoon as soon as we have a chance to chat. Back in our heyday, this building was filled with managers, clerks, reps, and salespeople." She pointed to different areas down the hall. "That was marketing, over there was the sales team, and down at the end was human resources." She sighed.

"Today, it's a different story. I've outsourced nearly everything, and the few new hires get to work from home. Sometimes, you need to suffer through a little short-term pain for long-term security. The truth is that times change, and we each need to do what we must to survive. It's an important lesson and a powerful instinct." She looked around the empty space and motioned for Elle to follow her as her footsteps echoed down the hall.

"There's no need for a space like this. It's so damn expensive to keep up, too. In fact, I'm thinking about selling the entire building. It's not an easy decision, but one that must be made. It turns out, they want to build even more lofts in the district. Who the hell can afford all these lofts? There aren't that many people in St. Andrews."

"I'd guess that loft dwellers like to drink, though?"

"They do, but they want a local IPA or cider made in their second cousin's basement. It's all about the made-locally bragging rights, I guess. When I first married into the business, McLeane focused exclusively on distribution. We got Kirk and most of the restaurants on the island their favorite poisons. Let's grab those two chairs near the front." She pointed at a pair of plantation lounge chairs framing the room's only window.

Effie lowered herself into one of the chairs, dropped her bag to the floor, and rubbed her hands together. "Then the market started changing; people started buying direct or off the Internet. So, we had our own little brewery for a while. Turns out, that's a lot of work. Let someone else make it, and I'll just sell it." She ended with a hearty laugh.

"Is that those the machines I hear in the background?" Elle asked.

"Yup, but I no longer have to worry about them. I'm leasing out the space and the equipment to a pair of hipsters who are trying to make their mark. I find them insufferable, but they haven't missed too many lease payments. The world keeps changing, but I've always been a survivor. I think it's an instinct you're born with."

She sat forward and focused her eyes on her guest. "So, is it Elle or Ellie?"

"Elle is fine, but I answer to either," she replied, opening her leather folio.

"Short for Elizabeth?"

"Actually, it's Elspeth. My parents came over from Scotland just before I was born."

"Oh, I've known your mother for years. You can't own a business here on Eagle Island without knowing Vee, and I also know that you and I have met time and time again. Never really talked at any length, but I'd certainly know you by sight. Although I think I already know, I thought I'd ask: what I can do for you, Elspeth?"

"You've heard about the book?"

"Orna Gunn made sure of that. In fact, I've had six different women reach out, each hoping to break the news to me. All but Orna hung up disappointed."

"Then I'm guessing you already heard about Peg Kinnear?"

"Absolute insanity," the woman replied with a shake of her head. "First, the Scott boy and now Peg. I'd hate to think of it as more than coincidence. I'd blame all this crime on the influx of loft dwellers, but the islands have always been this way. From one generation to the next, we simply choose to forget."

"I am searching a little further back than that," Elle noted. She could feel the older woman directing the conversation, and she wanted to take back the reins to keep the focus on her research.

"Orna mentioned you were asking about Shona Mackay. I'm happy to tell you what I remember."

"Anything you can offer would be appreciated."

Effie nodded and stretched in her seat. "Back about ten or twelve years ago, I first met Peg when she married Kirk Kinnear.

We were the bar's distributor, and I had known Kirk since I first moved to St. Andrews myself. Then Peg joined the local chapter of the American Dames, so we ran in the same circles for a while. I never cared much for all the Dames' genealogy stuff, but it made for good networking.

"Shona had moved next door to Peg and Kirk, so they naturally became acquainted. Within a month or two, Shona was helping with the bar's bookkeeping. Kirk simply raved about her, and I know it took a burden off Peg's shoulders."

"Did she eventually work for you?"

"She did. Very competent, from what I understand. I didn't work with her directly, though. We had a full-time office manager then, and she handled Shona's workload. Had there been any question at all about her work, I'm sure I would have heard."

"Can you tell me anything about the day Shona died?"

"Virtually nothing, I'm afraid. I was speaking at a conference in Atlanta. That afternoon, Peg had sent me a few panicked texts. Shona's death had left her absolutely mommucked. She was beside herself. Even as a married woman, she was terrified to be in that house. I think she kept Kirk's pistol under her pillow for over a month. It was another few weeks or so before she could get a good night's sleep.

"I will say, however, that I was proud of our local police. That could have been a nightmare had they not done such a thorough job of finding the guilty party. I applaud them for that." Her tone was clipped and decisive.

Elle nodded, admitting, "These kinds of crimes are always unsettling, and I suppose Peg did have something to worry about in the end."

"I have heard Orna's version, but I haven't gotten the official word," Effie said with a deep sigh. "Do they think it truly was an accident, or was it something more intentional?"

Elle shrugged and slid her pen back into its leather holder. "I don't think they can really tell at this point. If they know, I certainly haven't heard. Either way, it gives you pause to think."

"So very true. Not that it did Peg much good, but have you looked into owning a handgun?" the older woman asked with a stern expression.

Elle shook her head emphatically. "I don't like them at all. I know there are a hundred ways to ensure they are safe, but I never feel comfortable knowing they are in the house."

"I couldn't agree with you more," she replied as she opened and reached into her satchel. "This is what you need." From the bag she pulled out a blocky, oddly shaped plastic pistol with safety orange tips on one end. She handed it gently to Elle.

"Police tasers deliver about fifty thousand volts. I got this online, and it deals out several times that. Completely legal, too. Something I'd like you to think about. I've got your number, and I can text you the link."

Elle felt the heft and handed it back to her host. "Not a bad idea. For some reason, I also prefer a non-lethal alternative. I've made too many mistakes in the past, and it's good to know I can have a do-over if needed."

Deep in her host's canvas bag, a cellphone beeped. Effie fished it out, scanned her notifications, and fired off a pair of responses. "Even when I leave the office, I never truly leave the office. I hate to cut this short, but I now have even more errands to run before my dinner date."

"I appreciate the time," Elle offered as she rose to her feet. They walked to the broad door, Effie clicking off a bank of light switches.

"It's been my pleasure. One more thing I can offer, I'll talk to my CPA. He's been with me for twenty years. I'll ask if he ever had any unmentioned concerns about Shona's work. I doubt it, but who knows what may have crossed his mind." She gave Elle a handshake that was firm and exceptionally business-like.

"Tell your mother hello for me; it's been far too long. And when everything settles down, why don't we have lunch? My treat."

"I'd enjoy that," Elle replied as they stepped back into the afternoon sun.

The 400 block of Main Street in Saint Andrews was long known for the best selection of locally owned shops, eclectic cuisine, and personal services. As year-round island living had attracted a younger clientele, the tiny little district had worked hard to stay on trend. Over the past twenty years, a successful parade of art galleries, wine bars, and beachy boutiques had evolved into a colorful palette of bespoke clothing designers, regional makers markets, and farm-to-table gastropubs. Not everyone was happy with the change, but the district continued to thrive.

Elle made a quick stop by Books & Bottles to pick up a special-order Pinot Grigio for Lana and treat herself to another Mallory Swain period mystery. Since she was ahead of schedule—for once—she allowed herself the time to flip leisurely through a few more whodunnit paperbacks. The colorful, frenetic cover on the new Larry Givens caught her eye, while she passed over the latest mystery by her childhood friend Beatrice Bonnie. If *Murder in the Margins* was yet another Agatha

Christie pastiche like her last three, Elle would wait for the basic cable adaptation.

As she checked the bargain bin for anything worth the three-dollar risk, Elle heard a familiar voice at the register.

"Hello, Grady," she called over the stacks.

The older gentleman's bearded face peered around the magazine rack. In his right hand, he held a kraft paper-wrapped bottle, which he held up with a proud twinkle in his eye. "Despite today's tragedy, life must go on. I'm having a few friends for drinks this weekend. I know nothing of spirits outside of fine whisky, but Landon here was an invaluable resource."

The young man behind the register blushed at the compliment.

"I just wanted to thank you for your help with Kelsey," Elle said sincerely. "I never meant to antagonize him, but I think that ship has long since sailed."

"Sailed, caught fire, and sunk," he agreed. "Elle, I know today has just been a rough one, but I would like to talk to you if you've got a few minutes. I need to feed the dogs, but if you're not busy I could play host for an hour or so. I think we have a few things we need to discuss."

Elle gave the man a curious look, then nodded. "I'm free until dinner. Are you still out off Aberdeen Pike?"

"Last driveway on the left before you hit the river. I've also got something for you, or I should say, I've got something for Dan."

"Let me get this paid for. I'll see you in, say, twenty minutes?"

"I look forward to it," he replied as he tipped an imaginary hat.

19

But to see her was to love her, Love but her, and love forever.

— Robert Burns

During the short drive south out of St. Andrews, the oak trees grew sparse and far between as grass surrendered to scrub peppered with tickseed and wild buttonbush. The afternoon sun danced off the water to Elle's right while the surface of the Cape Fear River rippled beneath the coastal breeze.

Originally known as the Rio Jordan by sixteenth-century Spanish explorers, Cape Fear took its darker name in later years. Critical to settlement and trade in the region, the river proved a tricky thoroughfare for early English-speaking immigrants. Pirates, indigenous peoples, and hidden sand bars made water travel here a dangerous but tempting proposition.

Founded in the early 1700s to Eagle Island's north and east, Wilmington soon became a thriving center of trade and politics along the Carolina coast. Over the coming decades, towns like St. Andrews flourished as the region cemented its status as a major trade hub. Today, Elle's hometown still showcased that colonial-era history while an influx of construction erased older districts to make space for new developments. Even as wrecking crews razed centuries-old wharf buildings in favor of loft apartments, areas like south Eagle Island kept hold of their earlier roots.

Stretching all the way to the southernmost tip of Eagle Island, the grossly misnamed Aberdeen Pike—it was neither in Scotland nor had it ever been a toll road—degraded from weathered asphalt to crushed stone and shell. A single row of wooden power poles led Elle to where she turned left on the last private drive. Just beyond the corner nestled a tiny oasis of horse chestnut trees, cockspur hawthorns, and native white oaks.

Equal parts secluded and desolate, Grady Foster's edge of the island was dominated by a ramshackle Carolina beach house. Paint-stripped shutters hung listlessly on either side of open windows, while the covered veranda was festooned with lawn chairs, fishing gear, and crab traps. To the right of the main house, a double-carriage garage stood open to showcase a jumble of boxes, tools, and mechanical parts stacked inside.

While Elle pulled alongside the house, Grady stepped onto the front porch and waved her up. As she climbed the stairs to greet him, she looked out over the Cape Fear River. For a moment, she imagined she could see the stone house on Roan Island, the site of her recent fresh start that had gone tragically wrong.

Grady gave her a quick hug. "Thanks for driving all the way out here."

"It was no problem at all. After what happened to Peg, I was glad to get out of town for a few minutes. Plus, nothing on the island is really all that far from anything else." She looked around, taking in the breeze and the view. "I don't think I've been out here in fifteen or twenty years. Not since college."

"Has it been that long?" He shook his head and stroked his beard. "That would have been for the birthday party my wife and I threw for young Lyle MacUspaig, God rest his soul. That seems like only yesterday."

He pointed to the far side of the veranda. "We can sit out overlooking the water, if you like. Care for anything to drink?"

She shook her head. "I appreciate it, but I'm good. I've been talking to a number of people, and it always seems to involve coffee or tea or sweet tea. I should be well hydrated through summer."

He settled into an old wooden beach lounger and offered her another. "I've heard you're making the rounds. It all must have started right after Duncan met his maker."

"It did," she replied, accepting the offered chair. "I have a lot of questions and not nearly enough answers."

"I gathered as much," he nodded and thought for a moment. "I have a question or two for you as well. Would you be amenable to a trade? Your answers for my answers?"

"That sounds fair, Grady. Would you like to ask first?"

"Thank you, young lady." His eyes gave her a mischievous glimmer. "Now, I don't mean to sound impolite, but why were you in the Mackay house this morning?"

Elle had to laugh. "What gave me away?"

"As I closed the glass door—which I had shut myself just a few minutes before we left the first time—I experienced the pleasant yet distinctive aroma of pancakes and blueberry syrup. It was the second time this morning I had noticed the combination. My eyes aren't what they used to be, but my nose never lies."

"It's embarrassing," she began with a forced smile. She turned her eyes out to the ocean, buying herself just a moment as she felt her neck flush. "Dan and I were at breakfast when

Detective Tanner called. We came right over, and while he was telling us about poor Peg, nature called. The police wouldn't let me use either of the bathrooms at the Kinnear house, since I suppose it *is* the scene of an accident. So, Dan suggested I use the one next door. I saw you all leaving, and he assured me it would be fine. To be honest, when I saw the condition of Kelsey's bathroom, I changed my mind. I heard you both come back in, so I did what any reasonable person would do—I hid myself behind the television."

"That sounds plausible enough," he concluded. His sideways glance and gentle smirk suggested to Elle that he wasn't as convinced as he claimed. "One more question, then you are free to ask. Is young Jonah Tanner convinced that Peg was felled by simple misfortune, or does he believe that fate had a human hand?"

She considered her alternatives and opted for discretion. "He hasn't told me otherwise, so I'm sure he believes it was an accident. Do you?"

"Elle, when you're as old as I am, you learn there's only a hair's breadth of difference between fate and coincidence. Do I think that Peg Kinnear suffered an unimaginable accident? Yes, I do. Do I believe that she fell under the same riptide of ill karma we all currently struggle against? I do." With his admission, he relaxed back into the chair and gave his beard a few strokes.

"Ever since my dear Seonag died, the Mackay family and everyone connected to them has been mired in quicksand. Most, sadly, never know it. Some, like Kelsey, wear it on their sleeve like a badge of anger and vengeance. Others, like you and Peg, are caught up in the eddies and undercurrents that spiral around Clan Mackay."

"I don't know that I can disagree with you, Grady. Can I ask you a question about Kelsey?"

"My dear, you are free to ask anything you want."

"Has he found any peace at all in the passing years? I know what depression looks like, and I know how it feeds the anger. I've been there. I've spent far too much time there."

Grady looked out over the water and sorted through his thoughts. "Young Master Mackay has been drowning in his sorrow since the day his mother died. He's become an expert at surviving on regret and rage. It feeds him. As much as it pains me to say, I think the unfortunate death of Duncan Scott may be the key to freeing Kelsey from his bonds."

"Do you feel that Duncan's death was unfortunate?"

"I would never speak these words to either of Shona's boys, but I do. The loss of one life does not always demand the payment of another."

Elle watched as the old man continued to stroke his beard. His eyes looked lost both in thought and the past. "Just one last question. I have it on good authority that you would visit Duncan from time to time. In fact, you were the only person to visit him while he was incarcerated. Can I ask why?"

Grady sighed and took off his glasses. With the tail of his linen shirt, he gave the lenses a quick polish. He looked them over as he considered his words.

"I didn't go for the first year. I couldn't bring myself to look at him. The plea deal was the best possible outcome for everyone involved, but we had been robbed of a trial and the chance to witness the wheels of justice at work." He slid his glasses back into place, appearing to check his work for missed spots.

"At first, I just wanted to hear him admit his guilt. I wanted him to acknowledge the pain and loss he had caused through his selfish actions. Duncan, however, never wavered in his claims of innocence. He was steadfast in his denial of any part in Shona's death."

"Did you agree with him?"

"I never did. I know the lies we can tell ourselves when our own actions are too much to bear. Over time, though, I softened. Instead of simply blaming him, I wanted to understand him. I thought that if I could parse his thoughts and his intentions, I might be able to get on his wavelength. Perhaps then we could speak the same language. I could make him understand what he did to the family and the community. Duncan never gave me that satisfaction."

"What does your heart tell you happened between Duncan and Shona?"

"All I can assume is that Duncan was in love with Shona." He shook his head and looked out over the water. "I could certainly understand why. She was intelligent, kind, nurturing, and radiant—both inside and out. She had an open heart and a trusting soul, two beautiful qualities that may have led to her death."

"Why would he kill her?"

He rubbed his chin and looked out over the river and past Clarks Island. "I don't think we will ever know. I believe I knew her better than most, and she never so much as lifted a finger against another human being."

"How did the two of you meet?"

He smiled at the memory. "She and I were first acquainted a few years earlier. Peg Kinnear, God rest her soul, had recommended Shona to do a little audit work for my office when I was still with the chamber. It was nothing too complicated, just double-check the work of our volunteer bookkeeper. We were the heart of the town back then, and we sailed a tight ship.

"Once I got to know her, I couldn't help but fall in love. She had a beauty that was ageless and a heart as pure and open as the sea itself. Her voice had a light down-east twang that gave every word a delightful old-world charm. I never inquired about her first marriage, but I got the clear impression that she enjoyed living on her own. She had an independent spirit that I found irresistible. She was truly one of a kind."

"I'm sorry to bring all of this up," Elle offered gently, aware that she seemed to be stirring up old hurts all over the island. "I'm just trying to find some closure for the whole family."

"It feels good to talk about her after all this time. It's not something I ever dare to bring up with either of the boys." His face lit with a warm, melancholy smile. "Speaking of the boys, I almost forgot; I've got something for you to give Dan. I don't know if he'll want it, but I wanted to give him the choice."

Grady rose and disappeared into the house for a few minutes. He returned with a small photo, a faded snapshot of a sunny beach scene.

"I found this when I was helping Kelsey and Peg clean out Shona's garage after she died. For as long as we were together, I didn't have a single picture of Shona. She never liked having her picture taken. Every time we'd have a birthday party or Christmas morning, she would insist on being the one behind the camera. I always figured she was insecure like some women are as they get older. She had no reason to feel that way; she was always as beautiful as the day I met her."

He handed Elle the picture. A young Shona Mackay sat on a bench, her sunburned face surrounded by a halo of golden-red curls. Two older girls flanked her, one with large, almost comical sunglasses and the other with piercing blue eyes. Behind the three, a black and white lighthouse with a curious design of harlequin diamonds pierced the sky. She flipped it over. In a thin, blue script, someone had handwritten "Summer 1971."

"I don't know anything about the picture, just that the redhead must be Shona. Even without my glasses on, I'd recognize that hair anywhere. It was selfish of me, I understand that now, but I slipped it in my pocket. Kelsey was so protective of the pictures he had of his mother. I thought this was something God had hidden just for me."

"When Duncan showed up at Stirling Park, I think he had a copy of this photo in his hand."

"He may have," Grady replied. "A few months ago, I had come across the picture in my dresser drawer. I had a few duplicates made at the ValleyMart. I brought him a copy on one of our visits; I don't know what I was thinking. Maybe I was hoping that if he saw the picture, he might finally realize that it wasn't just Shona the woman he killed, but also this little girl who had never done anyone any harm."

"What did he say?" Elle asked.

Grady shrugged and lifted his glasses, rubbing his eyes with a free hand. "I don't know if I got through to him or not. He took one look and burst into tears, cried like an infant. The guard at the family yard finally asked me to leave. I left the photo with him. The next time I saw Duncan, maybe three weeks later, he never mentioned the photograph again. After his first reaction, I didn't want to pry."

"When was the last time you paid him a visit?"

"It was just about a month ago. His demeanor had changed. He was angry and restless, so I thought better of going back. I sent him a few letters, just my thoughts, but I don't know if he ever read them. And by the way, that photo is the original. I thought you could give it to Dan. I've got a copy for me, and I made one to give Kelsey someday."

"Is that where you left things with Duncan?"

"It was. I didn't hear he had been released until I got to Stirling Park on Saturday morning. He hadn't reached out to me. I think in the end, I was looking for the peace to forgive him for what he had done. I was never able to forgive him, but I was able to forgive myself for the anger I felt. My heart tells me that is close enough." He dabbed away a single tear and slid his glasses back down.

"That's enough time spent lamenting the past," he said at last. "Thanks for stopping by Elle, and I appreciate you delivering that picture to Dan."

The old man stood and looked at his watch. "I didn't realize it was quite this late. I've got company coming for dinner tomorrow night. First time I've done that since the wife died."

"I'll leave you to it," Elle stood and gave him a hug. "I appreciate everything you've done for Dan and Kelsey. They need your love and support."

"Yours, too, Elle."

20

Better to keep the devil at the door than have to turn him out of the house.

— Scottish Proverb

"Anyone still home?" Elle called out as she dropped her bag and leather folio on the chair inside the door.

"In here, Ellie," her sister replied. Lana stepped through the hallway door, working to close one earring. A loosely draped, dark blue halter top and tapered jeans perfectly balanced Lana's serious lawyer vibe with a sense that the office had closed for the day. "Sophie took the twins to Jungle Jenny's for a mommy and me pizza night. I've got dinner with Red and Anne MacFarlane plus a few more, so I had to beg off."

"Where are you all going?"

"New steak place next to Tierney's. It's a little on the pricey side, but I think Red is trying to impress me."

"Do you think he'd mind one more?"

"I could bring the twins and leave them with Red for an hour, he'd probably thank me. He is adamant that these new games take off. Duncan Scott has put a kink in those plans. What do you have in mind?"

"Just being nosey," Elle replied. "I didn't realize how connected Shona was to everyone here. She worked for Red for a while, so he may know something I might need."

"And it's a free dinner."

"That had completely slipped by me," Elle lied. She picked up her bag and folio and darted for the back bedroom. "Give me five minutes to change."

Red MacFarlane stood as the sisters entered the main dining room. Elle found the space to be typical for the newest wave of restaurants to grace the island. Industrial pendant lighting cast a soft light on small tables with simple settings and potted succulents. A chef's table dominated the far end with the open-concept kitchen bustling just beyond.

Red greeted them both and made quick introductions around the table. "Elle, this is a pleasant surprise. I think you both know everyone here." He was flanked by his wife, Anne, on one side and Preston Gilles of Highlands Construction on the other. Grier Hammond and Effie McLeane sat opposite them. As the sisters said their hellos, a waiter brought Elle an extra chair.

"I hope you don't mind that I brought a plus one," Lana entreated. "Her dinner date at Tierney's canceled at the last minute, so I asked her to tag along."

Elle gave an apologetic smile. "I usually would never crash a dinner like this, but Lana simply insisted."

"There's always room for one more," Anne exclaimed, her bright eyes widening with delight and, Elle felt, genuine enthusiasm. "In fact, Coira is one of our no-shows for the evening, so

Elle you can be the proxy for your boss. With your knowledge of our culture and history, I, for one, would love your input."

Shorter than her husband by eight or nine inches, Anne maintained a healthy, athletic figure well into her sixties. She had her long, expertly streaked hair tied back in a simple ponytail, and a pair of emerald stud earrings comprised her full choice of accessories. Elle had limited exposure to the woman since she first met her a few months ago. In that time, she found Anne to be friendly and inquisitive, a nice counterbalance to her husband's stiff, all-business demeanor. The woman struck Elle as a bundle of potential energy, always waiting for an opportunity to ask a question or dive into something new.

"Good to see you again so soon," Effie said, offering Elle the seat next to her.

"You, too?" Grier asked with a good-natured laugh. "Is there anyone you haven't talked to this week?"

"It's a small town," Elle replied with a playful shrug of her shoulders. "It really didn't take very long."

Red cleared his throat until he had the table's full attention. "I had thought about canceling tonight," he began. "I'm sure you've heard about Peg Kinnear."

As both sisters nodded, Anne broke into questions. "Do they know what happened yet? I heard it was a fall, but Enora Johnson swears it was no accident. She had been over last week to take Peg a cake, and she's saying now that something seemed off."

"Enora Johnson will usually swear that something felt 'off,' almost always in hindsight," Preston Gilles noted. In his early fifties, Preston was a robust man who looked accustomed to long days on a busy construction site. His tall frame was solid, if not athletic, and his dark brown hair and auburn beard had begun to show signs of gray.

"Well, Elle, you seem to know all the police in St. Andrews," Anne continued as Lana gave a snicker. "I wasn't sure if perhaps they had told you anything."

"Not so much as a word, Anne. I had seen her Saturday at the exhibition, then again on Monday. None of us could have guessed this would happen."

As Red ordered a bottle of wine for the table, Anne nodded and continued, "It's just that you have such a good sense for these kinds of things. I mean the sense you made of that mess on Roan Island…my head is still reeling."

"I heard about that little adventure," Effie commented. "That was an excellent bit of detective work, Elle. Nicely done."

"Thank you, Effie, but as of right now, I'm in the dark with the rest of you, I'm afraid," Elle replied. "When I spoke to her this week, we talked a little about Duncan Scott, but Peg kept bringing the conversation back around to Shona Mackay."

Red grumped and shook his head. "We've had enough death this week without the need to bring up another. As it is, the athletics exhibition has been completely forgotten as everyone can't keep quiet about who's been found dead where."

"I think with what happened to Duncan, Shona must have been on her mind," his wife interjected.

"That would make sense," Elle replied. After a moment she added, "And speaking of Shona, didn't she work for you for a while, Red?"

"Hmmm, she may have before we switched to the online bookkeeper."

"Red, she certainly did work for you," Anne corrected. "Grady Foster was using her for auditing, and Peg Kinnear gave her a glowing recommendation. You remember, dear, it was right before I quit working for the hospital in Wilmington."

"I think at some point, she may have worked for all of us," Preston added.

Grier shook her head. "She never worked for Sage Palm, but Grady always said she was absolutely tops."

"Actually, Grady is our other no-show for the evening," Anne said in an aside to the sisters. "I don't think we have any plans to add him to the board for the new games, but his announcing is such a landmark here on St. Andrews. Everyone simply expects it."

"I just left his place," Elle replied. "With everything going on around Peg, he may have just forgotten. It's been a difficult day for him. For all of us, really."

"How is he doing?" Grier asked.

"He was in a nostalgic mood. He seemed happier talking about the past and what once was."

"For some, that comes with our age," Effie noted. "Sentimentality makes for a comfortable cocoon."

Red cleared his throat for a second time. "Very true, very true," he replied as he turned his attention to his menu. "Now, ladies, I've heard that the hanger steak is excellent, but there really are no bad choices here."

Lana signaled and pulled onto Main as the sun was beginning to set. A crush of late-model sedans and SUVs fought for a dwindling number of empty parking spaces as mainland office workers stopped for a drink or a late bite to eat before returning home. Heading out of downtown, the traffic flowed with a steady rhythm.

"Did you get the same awkward feeling I did?" Elle asked.

"You mean about Shona?"

"Yup, that's the one. Red couldn't change the subject fast enough."

"There's a little history there," Lana explained. "Red has roving eyes. Grady is the same way, but when he does commit, he's strictly a one-woman man. Red, on the other hand, can't help himself. Or he won't help himself, whichever way you want to look at it."

"Really? He and Anne look so well matched."

"When I first started circling the board for these new games, Mama gave me a warning that left nothing to the imagination. Back a decade or so ago when she was soliciting Red's firm as a cleaning service, he was relentless. She reminded him, on more than one occasion, that she was packing and wasn't afraid to use it. He finally backed down, and she got the contract anyway."

"Never bet against Mama."

"Ain't that the damn truth. Well, supposedly, Shona got the same kind of attention when she started working for Red. She held her ground, but Kelsey caught wind of the situation. He had a few words with MacFarlane, and he wasn't subtle about it. He called him out in the middle of a crowd at one of the chamber's Burns Night dinners. From what I heard, Red backed off, but Shona quit soon after anyway."

"Poor Anne. I'd think she'd have better options available."

"Don't count her out," Lana replied with a snicker. "She's a smart one. After the Kelsey incident, word is she collected the evidence she could and lawyered up. I've heard she has him by the short hairs, and he knows it. She's keeping busy with tennis lessons and girls' trips and spa days. Meanwhile, he's keeping busy making sure she stays happy."

Turning the corner at Riverside Avenue, Elle's blood ran cold as Lana pulled over to let two police cars speed by. Her thoughts began to race as their red and blue lights bathed the surrounding houses in pulsating colors. Just as the cruisers disappeared around the turn to her street, Lana's phone began to buzz.

21

Who bravely dares must sometimes risk a fall.

— Tobias Smollett

Outside of the Cunningham-Klein home on Greene Lane, Sophie and Lana stood in the glare of the police car lights. Each held a twin while Elle finished a call with her mother. Angus sat patiently at her feet, watching the various police personnel walk by, sniffing each on the off chance of a treat.

"She had already heard from one of the women in dispatch," Elle said as she shook her head and dropped her phone in her pocket. "I told her to stay put, but I can promise you she isn't going to listen."

Officer Jeannie Pace spoke a few words into her shoulder com and approached the family.

"Tanner is off tonight, so I'll be taking this one," she began. "I just want to confirm that everyone is OK."

Sophie nodded. She looked understandably worried, her eyes moving systematically from dark window to dark window of her home. "I was bringing Izzy and Simon back from Jungle Jenny's and didn't even realize the lights were off. I thought Elle might have turned in early. I brought them both inside the kitchen. Angus was sleeping with his face in his food bowl. That's when I noticed the back door. I walked them out and put them in the car and called 911."

She began to shake as she spoke. "I was so terrified for Elle, and I didn't know what to do. Her car was here, but the lights were out. I wanted to find her, but I couldn't leave the twins. I am so sorry, Elle."

Elle swallowed the fear lodged in her throat and pulled her sister-in-law in for a hug. She couldn't even imagine how terrified, how vulnerable Sophie must have felt in such a helpless moment. She steeled her voice to reassure her. "You made the right choice, Sophie. Those two are your priority. I would have done the exact same thing."

As she spoke, Officer Glen Lewis came around from the side yard and holstered his service weapon.

"All clear," he said. "Looks like they stayed to one or two rooms."

"Can you tell if anything is missing?" Lana asked.

"I can't be sure until you all take a look. From what I could see, they jimmied the back door and went straight upstairs. Nothing looked touched except for the bedroom in the back."

"That's my room," Elle added. A chill crept down her spine as her initial fears were confirmed.

"They were looking for something important. Drawers and closets are open, and there are clothes and books everywhere. Looks like a bomb went off."

"In her defense," Lana replied, "that's how the room usually looks."

Glen laughed. "Unless she sleeps with the mattress propped up against the wall, then somebody went through that room with a mission."

"Mind if I take a look to see if anything is gone?" Elle asked, her mind racing and her sense of security pummeled by the intrusion.

"Can you promise me you won't touch anything? We normally wouldn't spend a lot of time on a break-in like this, but with everything else going on, there's no way this isn't connected." As he spoke, he opened the trunk of his cruiser and pulled out a black sports bag. From the bag, he extracted a pair of white latex gloves, tossing them to Elle.

"I'm not a crime scene expert, but these should help. Don't touch anything you don't have to, and let's keep it brief. I want you in and out through the back door. Just up to your room, a thirty-second scan, and then back here. Understood?"

"Understood," she replied as she slipped on the gloves.

Inside the house, the only light came from flashes of red and blue filtering in from the living room windows. She paused and listened for any unexpected sound, knowing the police had already cleared the home of any possible intruders.

As she turned the corner into her open bedroom, she realized she had been holding her breath. She gave a loud, slow exhale as she slumped against the doorframe. The room was, indeed, far worse than she had left it. The mattress had been lifted and propped against the far wall. Boxes of research materials had been upended and emptied on the floor. The dresser drawers were empty, with clothes separated into two unwieldy piles—which, Elle would later admit, was exactly as she had left them on laundry day. Her shoulder bag lay on the ground beside the bedroom door. A collection of papers, cosmetics, and personal items were strewn beside it.

Returning to the front yard, Elle removed the gloves and handed them to Officer Lewis. Far behind him, Lana and

Sophie each balanced a twin on one hip while Sophie conducted a cell phone call.

"The only thing I can't find is my leather folio." As she spoke, she realized the significance of that one missing item. It had been a bluff, really, just something to keep her hands busy during the interviews. Now, she thought, it had become something far more important.

"No chance it is buried under something?" he asked.

"It was in my shoulder bag when I got changed for dinner. The bag is empty, and the folio is nowhere around it."

"I'll let Tanner know."

As the officer returned to his patrol car, Lana approached her sister. She wrapped her free arm around Elle and laid her cheek on the top of her head. "You doing OK?" she asked.

Elle nodded and took a deep breath. "I'm OK, just have some bad news for you."

Lana stood straight for a moment then gave a tired laugh. "Worse than all this?" she asked, gesturing at the scene before them with a wave of one hand.

Elle sighed. "They took your leather folio."

Her older sister gave a deeper chuckle and hugged her sister close. "If that's all that's missing, we got off easy. I've got like four or five more of those things in my office closet. I'd think you'd be more worried about losing your notes."

Elle shook her head. "I haven't been writing most of this down," she admitted. "The folio was a nice prop. I thought it made me look more official for the book I kept telling everyone I was writing. It was mostly doodles. Everything of any value is either in my head or in the beat-up school notebook in my nightstand."

Lana nodded and gave Izzy a little bounce on her hip. "So, that's a good thing, then?"

Elle nodded and smiled. "Actually, that's a great thing. At least I know what the person was looking for. Even better, they didn't get what they wanted."

"Which means they might be back," her sister finished the thought. Her eyes read concern, Elle thought, despite her sister's endless reserves of bravery. "Ellie, I have a favor to ask of you. Please know that this is absolutely nothing personal. Sophie is really worried, and she and I feel it would be better…"

"If I stayed somewhere else for a few nights," Elle finished.

"You know we love you, but we are really scared for the kids."

"I haven't made a lot of progress this week, but someone else thinks I have. And if Peg's death wasn't an accident—"

"I think we can agree on that one now," Lana interjected.

"Then they are willing to take risks," Elle finished. She was sure of her convictions, even though the implications were too frightening to consider in detail. Elle watched as Sophie finished her call and came over to collect Izzy from her wife. The thought of anything happening to this family was too much to consider. It was only right that she do what she could to keep them out of harm's way.

"Did Lana talk to you?" Sophie asked.

Elle nodded. "I was thinking the same thing. And I'll pay to have the door fixed."

"Elle, let's just give it a few days. For the time being, I've already made us a room reservation at the Roanoke in Wilmington. I don't want any of us staying here tonight."

"Also, baby girl, I called Mama on your behalf, and she'd love the company."

22

The middle of life is the testing-ground of character and strength.

— Margaret Oliphant

After Officer Pace cleared the scene, Elle pulled together an overnight bag of essentials and drove to Douglas Drive. Vee was standing at the front door waiting for her when she pulled in behind her mother's car. As she and Angus reached the front doorstep, Vee kissed her on the forehead and gave her a hug.

"I'm just glad you're all right," she said in soft tones. She stepped back and looked her daughter in the eye. "Let's go inside. How is everyone else?"

Elle stepped into her mother's foyer as Vee locked the door behind her and armed the alarm system.

"I'd say it's late, and we can talk tomorrow," Vee began, "but I'm too riled up. Let's have something to drink. How about some hot cocoa and a little Irish crème?"

"I'd love some." Elle dropped her overnight bag next to the kitchen door and pointed her mother to a kitchen stool. "I got this."

"You think this is the first time one of you has come home to Mama in the middle of the night? Ellie, dear, it's already made. You can add your own Irish crème."

"It's 9:30. I'd hardly call that the middle of the night."

"At my age, anything that happens after Jeopardy is in the middle of the night."

Five minutes later, the two women sat on opposite ends of the guest room bed, sipping hot cocoa and finishing a shared package of digestible biscuits. Angus lay at Elle's feet, gently snoring and running in his sleep.

"I didn't mean to take you away from your scrapbooking. I know Thursday night is always scrapbooking time. You know, Mama, you've been putting together these scrapbooks for thirty years, and I don't think I've ever seen one of them. Lana swears they don't exist."

Vee clucked her tongue. "The books are for later. Someday when I'm gone, you'll have everything in those books to remember me by."

"Mama, I've never even been in your scrapbooking room. You've got it locked up like Fort Knox." She unzipped the suitcase and made stacks of clothes and toiletries on the wide, low dresser. Five full outfits should last her the full length of her exile, she hoped.

"That's your mother's sanctum sanctorum," Vee replied. "And please, put those in the drawers; that's what they are there for.

"With you two girls, your friends, husbands, wives, and children, that room is my oasis. I can sit and read or work on my books or simply do nothing at all. If you ever have a family that keeps growing like this, you'll understand what I mean."

"I get the appeal of a room like that," Elle agreed, continuing to make stacks across the dresser. "Although I'm not sure a big family like this is in the cards for me."

"Don't count yourself out yet, Ellie. I'm old enough to know that life can take you in unexpected directions. You've got me, and you've got Lana and her beautiful family. I'd even consider Dan and Paige a part of your clan, despite the mistakes you both made." As Elle zipped up the suitcase and stowed it in the closet, Vee quickly stood and began filling the dresser drawers with loose clothing.

"It never hurts to have a little help. Speaking of help, let's go downstairs. I want more cocoa, and I've got something I want to show you."

Seated at Vee's dining room table, Elle took the banded accordion file her mother handed her. The faded brown cardboard bulged at the seams as corners of accounting ledger sheets tried to escape the aged white string holding them all in place.

"Mama, what is this, and where exactly did you get it?" Elle demanded as she eyed her mother with suspicion

"You don't need that tone, Elle," her mother grumbled. "I went to a lot of trouble to get this for you. All in a Row still has the contract for the space on Fielding that Shona used to share with her bookkeeping partners. Sandy Buchanan does the night cleaning there, and she's a sharp cookie. With a little help from me, she was able to find where Shona's old files were stored. They'll usually have them for at least seven years for tax purposes."

Shocked at her mother's audacity, Elle shook her head and gasped, "You didn't, Mama."

"I most certainly did, and I'd do it again if I had to. We found the last three years of ledgers for Kirk & the Tartans. They were in an unlocked filing cabinet. Literally anyone could have gotten to them."

"And anyone turned out to be you?"

"Well, me and Sandy Buchanan," her mother replied with a satisfied smirk.

"All this time, someone has been following me to see what I know."

"You're right, Ellie. And they were keeping an eye on the wrong Cunningham."

"They certainly were." Elle laughed as she untied the file and pulled out a stack of loose pages. "I assume you've already looked through these. I have no idea how to read accounting sheets."

"I spent some time with them this afternoon after the news. As you know, I taught myself how to do my own books after I founded All in a Row Maid Services. In a real-world setting, hiding and moving money isn't that hard when you know what you're doing. I'm not an expert, but my guess is that Shona knew exactly what she was doing."

"What did you find?"

"I don't have all the pieces, but my sense tells me that the bar wasn't doing nearly as well as everyone believed. At least on paper, it doesn't appear to have been. Money was flowing in, but it was flowing out even quicker. I know they weren't numbers people, but I feel bad for Kirk and Peg if they didn't see it. One day, they're flush with profits, and the next, they are barely keeping their heads above water."

"Can you give me anything specific?"

She shook her head. "Nothing more than that, I'm afraid. There is another piece that I'm missing, and I don't even know what that piece might be. A forensic auditor might have an easier time with it, but then you'd have to explain just how you got these ledgers." Vee gave her a furrowed look and a wink.

"So, we can't even be sure Shona was up to something or not," Elle concluded.

"I can just suggest that this may be one part of the puzzle. We can't in any way loop Shona into this. And that's not the kind of accusation that should be made lightly, former family or not."

"Agreed." Elle sighed as she returned the sheets to the accordion file.

"I'll have Sandy put these back before anyone misses them," her mother said. "Speaking of missing, what was in that leather folio of yours? Are you sure it was taken?"

"I'm sure. When I packed for the week, I did a thorough check of the room. It's a good-sized folder and shouldn't be hard to miss."

"What did they get?"

"Several pages of doodles plus sheet after sheet of a genealogical project I was working on for Coira. Fortunately, I had copies of all of it."

Vee chuckled. "Somebody went to a lot of trouble for very little return. They must be feeling very foolish."

"Or very angry," Elle concluded.

As the grandfather clock in the front hall chimed eleven, Elle lay in the middle of her mother's guest bed and watched the ceiling fan spin. Her mind replayed the conversations of the past few days. Despite the suggestion of common themes running through each narrative, Elle knew she was missing the bigger picture. Perhaps she was too close to it, only seeing the fine detail of each thread and not the beauty of the tapestry. She jumped from Duncan Scott to Shona Mackay and back again. There were a dozen different connections from one victim to the next, but she didn't know where to focus her energy.

The clock struck 11:30, and the screen of her phone flashed in the darkness. She picked it up from the nightstand and checked her notifications. The screen flashed again alerting her to a voicemail transcription from Grady Foster.

Elle. I've been thinking, and I've had a change of heart. Call me tomorrow. Much love. Grady

She replaced the phone and focused on the spin of the ceiling fan. After a few minutes, her phone flashed again. She was tempted to ignore it. Grady, she thought, could wait until the morning. A third flash roused her to action. The screen showed two messages, not from Grady but from Dan.

Don't know if ur still up

Been thinking about u

Elle closed the bedroom door and swiped her phone open. She flipped a few screens and hit Dan's number. After a single ring, he answered.

"Hey, Ellie. I hope I didn't wake you."

"It's all right," she replied. The sound of his voice began to calm her overactive mind. "I couldn't sleep. How are you doing?"

"OK. Not great, but OK. Paige and I had dinner with Kelsey. It wasn't really a happy meal, but at least he's reaching out to me a little."

"That's a positive step."

"Yeah. We were finishing up, and Deedee Morrison asked if everything was OK with Lana's house. That totally caught me off guard, so she told me what she knew. I think she was pleased with herself that she knew before I did."

"Dan, I'm sorry I didn't call you. It came out of nowhere, and I'm going to stay with Mama for a few days."

"It's nothing like that, Ellie," he replied quickly. "I'm not your emergency contact anymore. I just wanted to make sure you and the family were all right."

"Sophie and Lana are more than a little shaken, but I'm fine. It's not the worst thing that could have happened."

"How's Angus?"

"Better than ever. Probably slept through the whole thing. He's one hell of a watchdog. Is everything good with you and Paige?"

Elle thought she could hear him pause and think for a moment. "Big picture? We are fine. Everything just rolls off her back like water. Me? I'm probably fine, too. I've been thinking about past mistakes and how I keep making them."

"Been there, Dan. Most days, I'm still right there."

"My biggest regret this week is telling you to drop all of this. It hurt, a lot. I didn't want to hear it because hearing it made me think about Mom. I'm further along than Kelsey may ever be, but there's more hurt than you know still churning inside me."

Elle sighed against a pang of regret and gently insisted, "I wasn't trying to bring that hurt to the surface, Dan."

"I know that. I always do. Not dealing with it was just easier. Now, with everything that's been going on with Peg Kinnear, with Lana's house, even your car, I know you are like a bloodhound on a trail."

"And someone out there doesn't like dogs."

Dan chuckled. "Exactly. And I'm hoping they have no idea just how good you are. It's not helping me sleep at night, but it might be the time to pull off this band-aid. God only knows what you're going to find and how little I will want to hear it, but I know you *are* going to find it."

"I don't have your faith." Elle took a deep breath to loosen the anxiety tightening her chest before letting the truth spill out. "I've been lying here for the past hour trying to shake everything over and over until it all makes a picture. There are so many pieces and broken fragments that don't make sense. I've got no real plan for tomorrow, so I might just take the weekend off to cool down and regroup."

"Well, I believe in you."

"Thank you, Dan. I needed to hear that."

He paused again. "And while I'm in the mood for some apologizing, I don't think I've ever said I'm truly sorry for what I did with Tammy."

"Let me go first this time," Elle cut in. She was grateful for the opportunity to finally get this off her chest. "I never apologized for shutting you out. We had a good start, and I wasn't ready for that kind of openness. We got too close too fast, and it scared the hell out of me."

"Apology accepted and appreciated. Again, Elle, I am truly sorry for everything with Tammy. It was a stupid decision, and I know how much it hurt you. It hurt Paige, too. That's not the kind of man or father I want to be."

"Apology accepted, Dan. If you don't mind me asking, what happened to Tammy? After the unfortunate incident with my truck and her hatchback, I didn't see much of her. Of course, that may have just been the restraining order, but she just disappeared with the wind."

"Well, it wasn't so much disappeared as left town in fear for her life," he replied. "You really put the fear of God into her. After you took that guilty plea, I think her choices were either another restraining order or just hightail it out. She opted for the second, which was probably the best decision she'd made all year."

"She's been a ghost since then?"

"Not so much as a whisper. I've seen her name on a few of the athletics point boards online. She must be competing out west or up north. There's no reason for us to ever stay in touch. I'm pretty sure she regrets ever getting involved with me. And speaking of regrets, you mentioned something the other day that really stuck with me."

"What was that?"

"You said how you regret not meeting Mom. I think you would have really liked her. She was funny and smart and clever. You two would have had a good time together; you both have a nose for sniffing out mischief."

"They say a boy marries his mother," Elle replied with a laugh. "Since we're on the subject of past mistakes, was Becky anything like Shona?"

It was Dan's turn to laugh. "God, no. Becky was…maybe still is…pretty and vacuous. She was empty of thoughts and new ideas. Lots of opinions on everything, but no spark or creative spirit.

"On my wedding day, my first wedding day, Mom was honest with me. She loved me and respected my choices, even if my current choice was Becky. We sat outside the chapel before the service, and she held my hand." His voice gave the tiniest break at the memory. "'I know today is a special day, but Lord knows, I'll be quamished 'til it's over. I also know that you'll be good for her.'"

"I'm glad you have those memories of her, Dan." Elle paused for a moment. "Do you want to know what Mama said to me on our wedding day?"

"I'm almost afraid to ask."

"I was getting dressed, and she turned to the entire bridal party. 'Are we certain Daniel knows what he's signed up for?'"

23

It's not the sort of night for bed, anyhow.

— Kenneth Grahame

That night, Elle dreamt of a sunny, watercolor beach scene in faded colors and soft lines. As she walked along the surf's edge, couples and families floated past without acknowledging her. The sun was faint and warm on her skin, and in the distance, the sound of waves overlapped the cries of seagulls creating a gentle, rhythmic harmony.

On the sand near the water sat a girl, perhaps ten or eleven years old. She wore a modest frilled bathing suit in seafoam green with oversized flip-flops that Elle imagined once belonged to an older sibling. Elle couldn't see her face, but the child's auburn curls rippled in the breeze like a slow-burning fire. Her hands dug at the sand, which she piled into small mountains, hills, and castles. Each wave brought the water closer to her little kingdom, threatening her creations with ruin.

Elle was startled when the girl turned to watch her approach. Of the dozen or so people on the beach, the child was the only one who seemed aware of Elle's presence. Her eyes suggested a soul that was both innocent and world-weary. Her smile was warm but tinged with an undefined sadness.

"Hello," the girl said at last.

"Hello. Where are your parents?" Elle leaned forward for a better look at the young girl's face.

The girl looked around and shook her head. "I don't know. I came here with my mother. She was down to the water. But when I looked for her, she weren't there."

"What are you making?" Elle asked.

The girl shrugged and went back to her digging. "I don't know yet. Right now, I'm just digging to see what I find." Her voice was soft and melodic with elongated vowels and slightly exaggerated burrs. To Elle, it sounded like the dying remnants of some English dialect from the Old World.

"What are you hoping to find?" She crouched beside the girl to see if anything was visible amid the clumps of wet sand and broken seashells.

"It's a secret," the girl replied after a pause. She frowned as her worried eyes darted around her.

"If you want, you can tell me."

The girl thought for a moment, then motioned Elle in with a curled finger. Elle leaned in to the child, bringing her cheek near the girl's mouth. The child spoke in a soft whisper, but the words never reached Elle's ear. Elle awoke with a start, the grandfather clock chiming five in the morning.

Friday morning, Elle lay in bed until the clock chimed seven. Two hours of silent contemplation had given her clarity but also more questions that needed answers. In every scenario, her thoughts came back to the odd little family with which she had been gifted. Her mother, the Cunningham-Kleins, and even Dan and Paige Mackay were now an essential part of her day. She had never thought of herself as someone who built or nurtured interpersonal bridges, but they refused to give up on her, even in those times when she had given up on herself.

Five minutes later, her phone began to buzz, first with a text message and then with a phone call. Lana's name on the notification was the only reason she answered.

"I was just thinking about you."

"Hey, baby girl. How was your first night back with Mama?"

"Pretty low-key. We drank cocoa and watched *Cold Crime Exposé*, then I went to bed early. Is everything OK with the family?"

"We are just taking this as an impromptu vacation. We took both cars last night because I knew today had a few bumps in it. The Roanoke has a nice pool and a few slides, so Sophie canceled her appointments for the day. I've got some paperwork to pick up at the office, then I'm driving back over to Wilmington. Which leads me to this call. I was wondering if you wanted to grab a late coffee or an early lunch before I head back."

"I can do you one better. If you want to leave your car here, I'll drive you back. I've got some research to do at the library there. We can get some coffee, and I'll be your chauffeur for the morning."

"Sounds like a good deal," Lana replied. "It's less hotel parking I'll have to pay for, too. I can run by the office first. Meet me at our house at nine?"

"Perfect."

"Are you going to tell me what you're looking for?" she asked.

"Not yet. That way, if I'm wrong, no one knows but me."

Even in the worst of traffic, the trip to the New Hanover County Public Library ran less than half an hour. Two coffees and a chocolate croissant later, Elle and Lana were merging onto Highway 17 and heading to the mainland.

Elle broke the ice. "How is Sophie? I don't want her to regret having me stay with you all."

Lana shook her head emphatically. "Lord, no. She is just thinking about the twins. She's got a strong mama bear instinct. She's also worried about you, Ellie. Last night, she said it was like the release you get after a scary movie. The immediate threat has passed, but you still have electricity coursing through your blood. If anything, I think she was relieved it was just a break-in. She's glad whomever it is tipped their hand a bit early."

"True, but that doesn't mean they can't come back for more."

"Of course, they can, but they flubbed it the first time. Now you know to be ready for them."

As Elle turned onto South 3rd Street, her sister picked up the old photograph laying on the center console. Lana let out a whistle. "I won't need two guesses to tell you which one is Shona." She studied the other two girls closely. "Damn, baby girl, is the one on the left Peg Kinnear?"

Elle stopped at a red light and took a closer look at the photo. The girl on the left did resemble Peg. She had the same slight build and birdlike bone structure. Her ice-blue eyes, though, were the giveaway. It was the dead woman in a younger, happier time.

"Damn. I hadn't even thought about it, but you're right." She paused as her thoughts fell into place. "It's odd, though.

Everyone I've spoken to says the two didn't meet until Shona moved to St. Andrews."

"Do you think they were friends?" Lana asked, flipping the photo over. "All three of the girls have the same smile and almost the same style bathing suits. I'd guess sisters or at least cousins."

"If so, then that's something even Dan didn't know. And for that matter, who is the older girl? I looked, and there's nothing on the back but the date, and according to Grady, it's the original."

"Is that where you got it from?"

"He found it in Shona's garage after her death. He's been holding onto it in memoriam. He told me to give this one to Dan. Damn."

"Again? What is it?"

"Grady called me last night. Remind me to call him when I get to the library. So, do you want to go with me, or should I drop you off at the hotel?"

"I don't mind a little break at the library. How about you do your thing, we can grab lunch, and I'll get Sophie and the twins something to go."

"It's a deal." Elle slipped the photo into her shirt pocket and turned onto College Road.

Elle found a shaded spot in the corner of the library's lot, and the sisters parted ways in the building's atrium. As Elle headed for the research desk, Lana disappeared into the stacks. For a small local branch, the library boasted a large central space with clerestory windows that flooded the room with diffused light. A dozen or more adults claimed the cluster of desks that split the shelves, while a group of children enjoyed story time in the colorful, glass-enclosed activity room.

Despite the presence of a main library only a few minutes away, Elle preferred to do her research at the southernmost branch. The space was quieter, easier to navigate, and staffed by a few of the best researchers she'd ever had the pleasure to work with. Best of all, the digital age meant that the lion's share of documents to be found at the larger complex could be accessed via computers nearly anywhere.

A diminutive woman with an asymmetrical, purple-tinged fade cut welcomed Elle with open arms. The young librarian's clothing was demure, almost dowdy, but the multiple piercings and the tattoos peeking over the high-buttoned collar suggested there was something more to her than met the eye.

"Happy Friday, Rosa," Elle greeted her. "Thanks again for the emergency assist."

Rosa waved off the concern. "This week, I'm on the periodicals desk. We don't get a lot of emergencies over there. Everything else on my plate can wait. I did a little preemptive research after I got your email this morning. We're going to need to start in Genealogy then come back here to Periodicals. In fact, we might have to make a few trips."

"Solid plan." Elle nodded as she pulled a spiral notebook from her bag. She opened to the fourth page. "I don't have much to go on, but I've listed everything in two stacks. Column A is everything I know for certain; Column B is what I needed to confirm or get rid of."

Rosa took the book and gave the two lists a quick read. "Some of this will be searchable. The rest is going to be looking for a needle in the proverbial haystack. Let's see what we can move from Column B to Column A."

Two hours later, Rosa had made a bundle of paper copies from the digital archives. Elle rubbed her eyes and filed the papers away in her shoulder bag. The librarian crossed two more items off Column B and made a photocopy of the list.

"I'll keep this copy," she said. "Friday afternoons are usually quiet, so if I get some time, I'll keep digging. I'll give you a call if I find anything worthwhile."

"You're a rock star, Rosa," Elle replied. "If you don't, it can wait. Lana and the family are taking a few days off over here, so I may come back in tomorrow. Until the boss gets back next week, my schedule is open."

Elle searched the stacks for her older sister. She checked Romance, History, and Politics—Lana's usual go-tos. Ten minutes later, she spotted her sister in the activity room. Lana was sitting cross-legged in the back of the group, focusing intently as an older woman read a group of children *The Adventures of Rosa & the Spectracles*. While the children laughed, her sister clapped and chatted with other mothers and fathers. Elle waved from behind the glass wall, and for a few seconds, she imagined that Lana was ignoring her.

"I am telling Sophie about this," Lana said at last after slipping out of the room. "I don't know who this woman is, but she does the voices better than Mama does."

Elle shivered at the thought. "Please don't let Mama hear you say that. They'll never hear from that poor librarian again."

"Did you find what you were looking for?" Lana asked.

"Yes and no. I found some of it, but there are a few blanks that need to be filled. If Rosa can't find everything, I may come back in tomorrow."

"Still not going to tell me what you know?"

"Not yet. I want to be 100% sure before I start making any accusations."

After the café waitress took their order, Elle remembered she hadn't yet returned Grady's message. She excused herself from the table and placed the call from the bench on the sidewalk. After five rings, the old man's voice requested that she leave a message. Elle was certain that she was talking to an old-school answering machine.

"Grady, it's Elle. So sorry I missed you. I got your message last night, and today has just been bonkers. I am in Wilmington for a bit but heading back to St. Andrews after lunch. Call me any time, or I can meet you in town or at your place."

"Any luck?" Lana asked as Elle joined her at the table.

"No, and I'm not sure what he needed. He called me last night to say he'd had a change of heart about something."

Lana spread a little butter on a complimentary sesame cracker and spoke around bites. "Ellie, I've been thinking. Let's say that Shona, Peg, and the third girl are related or friends or whatever. They are connected. My first thought is that we need to find the sunglasses girl. Someone has targeted the first two, and she would be the logical third."

"I was having the same thought," Elle replied. "If someone *is* targeting them, one question would be *why*. If we knew that, maybe we could figure out who she is or even where she lives. That raises another question. Maybe she's already dead; maybe whoever this is already got to her. Shona's murder was five years ago, so it's certainly not out of the question."

"And that leads you to another question. Why does no one know—or admit to knowing—that Shona and Peg were connected since childhood? What were they running from, and how did it find them?"

Elle sighed and picked at her summer salad. "Once I find my answers, and I think I will, how will I break all of this to Dan?"

Lana skewered a strawberry from Elle's plate and popped it in her mouth. "I didn't want to be the first one to bring that up. There's not going to be an easy way. For me, the thorniest Pandora's box is Duncan Scott. If you're right and he had nothing to do with Shona's murder, he went to jail for a crime he didn't commit. The last few years of his life were taken from him, and it may very well be why he was murdered. There's no easy way around that."

Elle set down her fork and dropped her napkin over the bowl, her stomach too twisted in knots to take another bite. "I'm losing my appetite. I know that I'm doing the right thing, but I also know how this is dragging Dan to hell and back. I don't want to cause him any pain, but these are life-and-death problems that aren't going away. Communication wasn't our strong suit. It was easier to ignore anything that didn't make us happy. You can see how that worked out."

"Do you want some big sisterly advice?"

"Everything you've learned from the two extra years you've spent on the planet?"

"Something like that. The trick to marriage—at least to my marriage—is communication. It's nice to like the same things. It's important to have the same values. It's even fine to have totally different personalities. The hard part is learning to communicate.

"A lot of that is just knowing when to listen and knowing when to shut up. It's not about speaking first or always being right; it's about making sure you both feel heard."

"I hear you," Elle replied.

Lana laughed. "See how easy that is?"

Elle parted ways with Lana at the Roanoke, dropping her sister off at the hotel's poolside gate. As Lana disappeared around the corner of the tall privacy wall, twin squeals of joy arose from the direction of the children's play area.

On Highway 74, Elle reviewed what she knew. She acknowledged that it wasn't much in the way of fact, more conjecture than anything. She hoped Rosa would have luck in the periodicals archive. As she drove back to St. Andrews, she gave Grady Foster's number another try. On the third ring, someone picked up.

"Hello?" a familiar voice asked.

"Jonah?" Elle replied. "Sorry, must have hit the wrong button. I meant to call Grady Foster."

"You got it right. I'm at Grady's place now."

Elle gasped. For a few silent moments, her mind raced through a dozen possibilities, each more grim than the one before. "Is he all right?"

"I honestly don't know," he replied. "No one has seen him since last night. His car is here, his keys are here, and the dogs are here. Everything is here except Grady."

"Damn. Damn. Damn," Elle said under her breath. "I should have taken his call."

"When did he call?"

"Last night. I think it was 11 or 11:30. I was already in bed, so I let it go to voicemail."

"Did he say what he wanted?" Elle thought she could hear the scratching of a pen on the pages of a tiny notebook.

"No. He said he'd had a change of heart or something like that. He didn't sound upset or panicked, just determined. I tried him before lunch but hadn't heard back."

"You and I were the only messages on his answering machine."

Elle let the silence hang for a moment. "No chance he went for a walk?"

"Not without the dogs. They were still in the house when I got here."

Elle's mind attempted to put the facts into logical order. She found comfort in Jonah's presence at Grady's oasis, a coincidence that piqued her interest. "Mind if I ask why you were stopping by?"

"Got a call from him last night, probably right after he tried you. We only talked for a minute; it was the same story. His conscience was nagging him a bit, and he needed to clear his head. We were going to meet for breakfast in town. He never showed, so I called, then drove down here to see if he was OK."

"I don't like this, Jonah."

"Neither do I. Everything in the house is exactly as it should be. There's no sign of a struggle. The lights are on; the television is on. Nothing has been disturbed. There's just no Grady."

"So, what do we do now?" she asked.

"We are doing two very different things," he replied in a stern tone. "I am going to talk to his neighbors and see if they know anything. You, on the other hand, are going to stay put at your mother's house. Are you there now?"

"On my way. Just dropped off Lana in Wilmington."

"Jeannie told me about their house." His voice shook ever so slightly as he spoke. He paused a moment before coming back with a warning. "Elle, this is not going to end well. If something has happened to Grady—and I'm not saying for certain something has—" He paused again and swallowed audibly, "if you throw in Roan Island, that would be seven confirmed murders on the islands in half as many months. We do that kind of number every three or four years. At this rate, by Christmas time, St. Andrews will be a ghost town."

"When we have a chance to talk, I have some thoughts I need to go over with you. It's not much, but it's a start."

"I'm glad you're staying busy, Elle, but I need you to reel it in. I have no problem admitting you were right. Yes, there is something much bigger to Duncan's murder. The reality is that whoever killed him, and maybe Peg Kinnear, and possibly Grady, is very likely, still out there. And you have already been in their sights twice. This just keeps getting messier.

"I'm not asking you; I'm telling you now is not the time for plans, schemes, farces, or whatever else you've been thinking of. I'll call you when we have time to talk this out. Get back to Vee's house and stay put. Will you promise me that?"

"I promise," she replied. She intended to keep her word.

24

How often have I said to you that when you have eliminated the impossible, whatever remains, however improbable, must be the truth?

— Sir Arthur Conan Doyle

As Elle pulled into her mother's narrow driveway, she finished leaving a voicemail for her ex-husband. She dashed off a quick text to Paige: "Things are getting weird. OK but weird. Just want you to know you mean the world to me. Talk to you tomorrow. <3 Aunt Elle."

She let the car idle for a moment as she called her mother. "When will you be home, Ellie?" Vee asked without saying hello. "I need to know what time to start the chicken."

"I'm out front, Mama."

"Then why are you calling me? Are you still in your car? You couldn't wait to come in the house?"

"Mama, grab your keys. I need you to swap places with me in the driveway. I'll explain in a second."

Vee gave an audible sigh. "I'm up in my scrapbooking room. Give me a chance to put this away, and I'll be down."

Five minutes later, the two women sat at the kitchen island as Elle cut squash into thin yellow disks, arranging them carefully in a casserole dish. Vee wrapped a baking pan of chicken breasts in aluminum foil. She shook her head and gave her daughter a concerned look.

"I believe you, Ellie. This has got me worried, and it takes a lot to worry me. You're developing a positive talent for finding trouble. It doesn't help me sleep at night. At the same time, I know I can't stop you from doing what you do."

"I'm not sleeping much, either. When Duncan was killed, I was just doing this for Dan. Then it was Dan and Paige. Now, I'm doing it for all of us. There is someone out there who doesn't mind seeing to it that others get hurt—or worse.

"Jonah is tied up in finishing this his way, and I understand that. I am just looking for the steps I can take to get to the answer faster."

"So, what is your next step?" her mother asked as she slipped the baking pan into the oven.

"I'm not a hundred percent sure, Mama. I think I know where this is going, but I need some confirmation first. Rosa at the Wilmington Library is doing some leg work for me. If she can't find the answers I need, I'll head back over tomorrow and pick up where I left off. Maybe take the kids off Sophie and Lana's hands for a bit."

As Elle washed her hands in the kitchen sink, she caught herself. Drying off her hands, she carefully pulled the old photo from her shirt pocket. She handed it to her mother.

"What do you make of this?" she asked.

"Such cute girls," Vee replied. "Who are they? I'd guess that little one is Shona Mackay."

"Good guess. And I think that the one with blue eyes might be Peg Kinnear."

Vee lifted her glasses from around her neck to better study the trio. "I'd say you're right, Ellie. Don't recognize the third girl, though. Where'd you get this?"

"Grady Foster gave it to me. He found it at Shona's place after she died. He wanted me to give it to Dan."

"Poor old Grady." Vee dropped her head into her hands and kneaded her brows. She shook her head before looking at Elle with sad eyes. "I hope that this is just a big misunderstanding. I hope they find him napping under some tree on the river."

"I hope so, too, Mama, but I'm worried he's not."

Her mother examined the photo one more time. "These girls look so happy and carefree. It's a shame to know that two of them are dead now. And to think how they met their ends." She handed the photo back and shook her head. "It gives me a shiver."

"What do you think, Mama? Could they be sisters?"

"They could be. Just the three of them on vacation with their parents. It was clearly a special photo if Shona kept it all these years. I can't imagine her holding onto it if they were just friends or distant kin."

"I agree with you on that," Elle replied. "I just don't know why Peg and Shona didn't mention this to anyone. Orna Gunn suggested that the two weren't very close, even as neighbors."

"That's such a shame," Vee lamented. "To have someone who knows you so close by and not to acknowledge it."

She turned to look at her daughter, taking a hand in hers. "Let me give you a little motherly advice, Ellie. Often in life, you find that all you have is family. Friends come and go, marriages blossom and fall, but family is forever. When I'm gone, you and Lana will be the last of this branch of the Cunninghams."

Elle stood and gave her mother's shoulders a hug. "First of all, you're going to outlive all of us. I feel that in my bones. Second, Lana will always have me. She'll have one hell of a time getting rid of me."

"Language, sweetheart," Vee replied. "One of my proudest accomplishments is that I've raised two smart, independent daughters, and that you two have the relationship that you do. I feel like I've done my work here. Not all families are this close. I would do absolutely anything for my girls."

As her mother returned her hug, Elle's phone began to vibrate. she snatched it off the island counter and answered the call.

"What did you find?" She rooted through the kitchen catch-all for a pen and paper. Her phone tucked under her ear, she found a dull pencil and old business card behind an outdated phonebook.

"I found an article about them," Rosa's voice answered on the other end. "It was a house fire. That led me to a few other documents. The missing name was Oighrig, pronounced 'OY-rick.'"

A flash of light exploded in the distant recesses of Elle's memory. Her excitement rising, Elle began to fill any available space on the business card with a scribble of tiny notes. "Can you spell that for me?"

"O-I-G-H-R-I-G." Elle took her notes and smiled.

"I made a scan, and I'll email everything to you for your notes."

"Got it. Rosa, you are amazing. I owe you one." She hung up and slipped the card into her pocket next to the photo.

"Did you get what you were looking for, Ellie?"

She nodded and tapped the pencil on the face of the cell phone. She picked up the phone and dashed off a quick text. "Mama, you said you'd do anything for your girls."

"Don't make me regret saying that."

"Too late. I'm going to need your house tonight, and you are going to be taking up Mahjong."

Vee dried and put away the last of the dishes from dinner as Elle's phone vibrated a second time that night. Elle checked the caller ID and flashed Vee a sly smile. "Here we go, Mama." She answered the call.

"Orna, thank you for calling. I wasn't sure you'd gotten my text," Elle gushed.

"Elle, how are you doing? Have you heard about poor Grady Foster? He's missing," she replied without waiting for an answer. "And I heard about the break-in from Anne MacFarlane and Enora Johnson. How absolutely dreadful for you."

"It was an absolute nightmare," Elle whispered, injecting a note of drama into the lie. "My entire room was turned upside down. They certainly did a thorough job of ransacking the place."

Orna gasped. "I do hope they didn't take anything."

"I think they were after my leather folio, you know the one I keep all my book notes in. Fortunately, whoever they are, they only got my extra binder, not the one with my notes."

The woman gave an audible sigh of relief. "What a stroke of luck! So, your notes are safe?"

"Orna, I'm hoping I can trust you with a secret."

"Of course, my dear, anything. I am the very model of discretion."

"I've got it with me at my mother's place. I decided to stay here for a few nights until the police are done with the other house."

"An excellent idea," the woman concurred.

"Thank you, Orna. Now, the reason I called you. I have made some excellent headway into this whole mess. Since you were there from the beginning, I thought you and I could have breakfast tomorrow and go over my private notes."

"Elle, darling, I'm sure I could free up my schedule." Through the phone, Elle could feel the woman's anticipation.

"Mama is out playing Mahjong tonight, so I'll have some quiet time to get my thoughts together. I want to get your expert opinion. How about Thistle Do Nicely at 9 a.m.?"

"I'll see you at 9 a.m. sharp!" Orna replied a bit too eagerly.

25

"I fear nothing when I am doing right," said Jack. "Then," said the lady in the red cap, "you are one of those who slay giants."

— Andrew Lang, *The Red Fairy Book*

As the sun dipped below the horizon, Elle took a second tour through the house. In each room, she extinguished the lights, closed the blinds, and drew the curtains. She double-checked the front door to make sure it was locked, then the back door to ensure it was unlocked. The alarm system flashed a steady green, indicating the system had yet to be armed for the night.

In the darkened living room, she took one last peek between the shuttered plantation blinds for any activity in the neighborhood. Her SUV sat alone in the narrow drive, and the street was empty of other cars and late-evening walkers.

A few minutes later, she retired to the guest bedroom. She sat at the small vanity, her back to the hallway door. The ceiling fan lamp overhead illuminated the room, the lights swaying ever so slightly as the blades spun out of perfect balance. Even though it was one floor and several rooms away, the grandfather clock ticked with the steady, calming rhythm of a metronome.

She passed the time working on a small research project for work. As she typed, she worried her mind wasn't up to the task; she'd likely have to proof every edit she'd made. Still, she thought, it kept her hands busy. As the grandfather clock chimed the quarter hours, her phone would vibrate every so often. When she checked her notifications, she acknowledged then ignored messages from Jonah and Dan. To a message from Lana, she simply replied with a quick <3.

As the clock marked the passing of 10:45, Elle began to question her strategy. The solution to the string of violent acts had been obvious in retrospect, although it left her with no clear path forward. With Jonah focused on the missing Grady Foster, she was temporarily on her own. Her plan for the evening was a Hail Mary—she recognized that—but it was also the only option she had developed.

She closed the screen of her laptop and leaned back in the vanity chair. Her back ached from holding an upright position in such a small, impractical seat. As she stood and stretched, her phone buzzed again. She let it go to voicemail. In the corner of her eye, she registered an out-of-place shadow. She turned to a stout woman's figure in the bedroom doorway.

"I hope you don't mind, but I let myself in," Effie McLeane said in a businesslike tone. "Orna let slip that you might be here by yourself with something new to share about your book."

She was dressed in a pair of dark jeans and a black hoodie. Her gray hair was tied back in a simple knot. In her extended right hand, she held a blocky black gun with bright orange tips. She used it to motion Elle back to a seated position.

"That's a sloppy way to kill someone," Elle replied as she lowered herself into the chair with the slightest tremor in her movement. Although keenly aware of the danger the weapon posed, she did her best to maintain a calm exterior.

"It's not ideal and certainly not lethal, but I've always been good at improvising. All part of that survival instinct that's carried me so far. This is effective up to thirty feet, but I won't need even half of that." She punctuated the boast with a flash of a grim smile.

"Plus, I think I'm past the point of being careful. I gave you several opportunities to settle down, but that doesn't seem to be in your DNA. Shame." Effie slowly entered the room, still pointing the stun gun at Elle.

"When you made it clear you'd never suffer a gun in your house, I thought this might be a good chance to wrap things up. Really, this will just be a stop-gap measure. A few good jolts, and I can follow up with a pair of contact charges. It won't kill you, but it will give me a few minutes to make up my mind. Strangling you will be easiest, by far. Or perhaps I just bludgeon you to death."

"Then why are you hesitating?"

"I have too many unanswered questions. Normally, I wouldn't care, but I'm curious what you've come up with."

Elle swallowed hard, hoping that she hadn't underestimated the woman's impulse for violence. But the fact that she wanted answers, too, meant she could be kept talking, as long as Elle played her cards right. She turned slowly in the chair and relaxed her back against the vanity. "What would you like to know?"

"What have you pieced together? And how?"

Elle smiled. "Well, I was curious about the death of Duncan Scott but more interested in what happened to Shona Mackay. For a variety of reasons, I felt that Duncan was innocent. Shona wasn't killed for her jewelry, otherwise, it wouldn't have been slipped by someone else into Duncan's work bag. So then, what was it? It had to be something worth killing for."

"And what, pray tell, did you decide that to be?"

"Usually, it's money," Elle answered.

"You're getting warmer." She gave another dark smile.

"It was a simple series of events. You come to town and are soon part of the MacLeane distribution business. Then Peg arrives and, after your introduction, marries Kirk Kinnear. Shona soon follows and is handling Kirk's books on Peg's recommendation. Nothing too suspicious on face value alone. But then this popular, lucrative bar is hemorrhaging cash and going under." The older woman nodded slowly.

"You three women—completely unconnected—had the perfect gigs as Kirk's distributor, wife, and bookkeeper. I'm guessing you saw a financial opportunity in old Kirk and just kept adding ringers until the game was stacked in your favor. You're providing invoices for deliveries that never happened, Peg's signing off on the checks, and Shona is balancing it all. Before long, he was broke, and all the money had simply disappeared."

Effie nodded slowly. "An interesting take, but you've got nothing but conjecture."

"And copies of the accounting books for Kirk's as the bar went under. A quick look indicates that the numbers don't add up as well as they should." It was Elle's turn to give a sly smile.

Effie's eyes narrowed as she sneered. "I don't believe you."

"It doesn't matter, does it? There is, however, one additional piece that helps tie it all together."

"And that is?"

"A picture Grady Foster found in Shona's garage. Three young girls enjoying a day at the beach."

Effie shook her head. "Damn. I thought I had the only copy. Duncan was waving it around at Stirling Park, but I never thought anyone would notice."

"There are other copies. I happen to have seen the original. The youngest girl is clearly Shona Mackay, the girl with blue eyes must be Peg Kinnear, and the third could very well be you. My guess? You all are sisters. It's odd since in the years you three have lived here, you've never mentioned it. It makes one ask what other secrets you all might have been keeping."

"That's a guess, at best. You must have something else."

"I have another guess. It was Peg who killed Shona. She had easy access to the house and the garage. She was likely one of the very few people who knew that Shona had switched bedrooms. She could come and go without Shona ever worrying. Perhaps she threatened her sister with her gun, tied her up, and strangled her. Shona was dead before Duncan and Orna ever showed up that morning. Plus, with Duncan at the house at Peg's request, she had an easy patsy and alibi. Simply drop the rings in his bag and let the police do the rest."

Effie gave a menacing chuckle. "You're wrong on one point. She didn't have to threaten Shona at all. Shona was never happy about our work milking Kirk and the bar; in fact, I don't think she ever really grasped the extent to which we were bleeding him dry." She took a single slow step further into the room and sighed.

"Shona always was the soft one. She began feeling guilty about the bar going under, but she never let on. Then Peg hears through Grier Hammond that our little sister is looking to sell. She was asking about comps in the neighborhood and thought there wouldn't be any harm in checking with Shona's neighbors."

"And that was reason enough to kill her?"

"Again, I've got an instinct for survival," Effie replied. "Shona's got a family, she's got a new man, and her conscience is catching up with her. She's trying to leave town, and she never mentions it to us. From that point on, she couldn't be trusted."

"How did Peg get her bound to the chair?"

Effie curled one end of her mouth into a vicious sneer. "That was another one of my ideas. Peg let on that she knew about Grier Hammond. Shona was mortified and begged her not to tell me. It was already too late as Peg had let me know the instant she found out. We both gave her our blessing. All she had to do was help us with a staged home invasion. We'd fake a robbery, make a few insurance claims against pieces Shona didn't own. I lent her several of my best, we had them insured, then I returned them to my safety deposit box. With the insurance payout, Peg and I would ostensibly put the money back into the bar, and we'd all go our merry way."

Elle shook her head, her eyes never leaving the weapon in the woman's hand. "Still, I can't see doing that to your own sister. It's unfathomable."

Effie waved the stun gun dismissively. "Despite what the greeting cards say, family isn't forever. In the end, you and you alone are the only person you can count on. Peg was terrified, but she was always a follower. She had more fear of me than she had love for Shona. Well, she had more fear of me, several years in prison, and losing her husband and her lifestyle. That kind of terror is a powerful motivator." Effie shook her head and smiled, more of a nasty grimace Elle thought. Her eyes were distant and disdainful.

"All Peg had to do was strangle Shona from behind—no need to even look her in the eye, slip the rings into Duncan's bag, and wait for him to discover the body. There was no chance he would wait around for the police."

She motioned Elle back to a standing position. "This has taken long enough. Let's get this over with."

Elle's heart skipped as she held up her hands. "You can't afford to yet," she insisted, trying not to let it sound like a plea.

Effie sighed. "That damn portfolio. I took far, far too many risks to come up empty handed. Let's have it."

"Just a few more questions, and it's yours."

Effie motioned with the stun gun. "Make it fast."

"Why Duncan, Peg, and Grady?"

"I thought everything was settled until Duncan got released. He came to Stirling Park, and I saw the photo in his hand. I had no idea where he had dug that one up. God knows, he wasn't the brightest boy, but I think he recognized my sisters in that snapshot. I don't think he was looking for Dan, but rather Peg. I couldn't take the chance that he'd get other, smarter people to ask the wrong kind of questions.

"After the scuffle, I knew how he'd be walking home, tail between his legs. I grabbed one of the pitchforks. It was total bad luck that the fork was Dan's. He was an early out, so it was just sitting there. I admit that was a mistake on my part. I was just another woman in a great kilt walking around with a pitchfork.

"I caught up with Duncan as he was leaning against that old stone gate, eating pistachios, and feeling sorry for himself. The pipe bands were playing, so there was no chance anyone would hear him. Oddly enough, he never made a sound. Just in and down. I never thought it'd be that easy."

"And Peg?"

"That was your fault, Elle. You started asking questions, and Peg just loved to talk. She would slip up sooner or later. I was surprised as hell she'd kept it together this long. Just walked to her house from the north field, and she offered me a piece of cake. She was cleaning the basement, so I offered to help. She came up with a box of books. She set them down, and I gave her a push backward. All I had to do was toss that box down after her to make sure she was dead."

"Your only living sister?" Elle asked, shaking her head in disbelief. Her stomach churned at the thought of that kind of betrayal.

"I'll say it again. I rely on myself and myself alone for survival. Peg was a sister, but, like Shona, she was also a threat. Between the insurance money from the bar and what we'd stashed away from Kirk's, we both tucked away nice little nest eggs. McLeane's has been on the downswing for several years, and I don't feel like keeping up with the younger generation. Peg has a will filed in Dare County. I'll let it rest in probate for a bit then head back home to claim what extra she has banked. It's not ideal, but I'd rather have the money than a sister who can't keep her mouth shut."

"But why Grady?"

"That was the only...incident...here I truly regret. From up in his booth, Grady saw me walking toward the north gate with Dan's pitchfork. It didn't take him long to piece together what had happened to Duncan. He reached out to me to confess what he saw. He thought it was some kind of revenge for Shona's death, and in the beginning, he actually thanked me.

"The sad thing is that he's a sentimental old soul. Sooner or later, his heart would catch up with him, and he'd say something I'd regret. In the years since Shona died, Grady had developed a soft spot for Duncan. Grady was a liability."

"Is he still alive?"

"No, I'm sorry to say. I paid him a visit early this morning. He was surprised to see me; he even took me out to the dock to watch the sunrise. One hammer blow, and he was in the water.

The tides were changing, so he would be out a ways before anyone came looking for him.

"And that just left you as the last loose end. So, let's have that binder. Hand it over, and I might let you live."

"But probably not," Elle replied.

Effie nodded. "Probably not."

Elle opened the vanity drawer and withdrew a manilla folder filled with loose sheets of paper.

"Throw it on the bed," Effie demanded, pointing with the stun gun.

Elle tossed the folder onto the corner of the chenille blanket covering the bed. "There's just one more thing you need to be sure of."

Effie sighed and leveled the stun gun at her target. "You have five seconds. One."

"Who else knows what I know?" she said, unable to stop the satisfied smile from spreading across her face.

Effie paused and blinked, her mouth curling into a slight sneer. "How the hell many people did you tell? Two."

"Just one," Elle replied.

"Just one? Three."

"Just one," Vee repeated from the hallway. She had her shoulder braced against the bedroom's open doorframe, and in both hands, a compact Ruger pistol targeted Effie McLeane's back. "Drop the taser, Effie. I'm not counting to five."

26

To be kind to all, to like many and love a few, to be needed and wanted by those we love, is certainly the nearest we can come to happiness.

— Mary, Queen of Scots

As Saturday morning broke with a light storm, Elle lay across the couch in her mother's den, a sleeping basset hound nestled up against her. Vee sat across from her daughter in an overstuffed leather chair. She gently stirred a cup of tea as she listened to the raindrops against the windows. She took a tentative sip and returned the cup to its saucer to let it cool.

"Still too hot?" Elle asked.

"I can't taste it if I don't have any tastebuds left," Vee replied. "How are you feeling this morning?"

"Tired. Relieved. Relaxed. A little of all three." As she spoke, Elle heard the front door open and close. Lana entered the room, her coat and hair wet from the early morning shower. She bent down to give her younger sister a hug.

"Dear, put that coat in the kitchen. I don't want all that water on the hardwood."

Lana kissed the top of her mother's head and left down the hall. "I just wanted to see how you two are doing," she called from the other room.

"Fine," Elle replied. "How's the family?"

Lana returned to the den, a cup of steeping tea in one hand. "They are fine. Mama gave me the Reader's Digest version last night after the police left. I think we are going to stay in Wilmington for another few days. It's the first real vacation we've had since Sophie merged her practice with the Vance group." She moved her sister's feet off the end of the sofa and took a seat. She jiggled the tea bag as she waited.

"Be careful, Lana, it's hot," her mother warned.

"That's how tea works, Mama," she countered with a smile. "While we're waiting for my tea to cool, I'm going to need a few more details."

"Shoot," Elle replied.

"Excellent word choice, baby girl. My big question is… actually, it's a two-parter… how did Mama know Effie had you at taser point?"

"I'll take this one, Ellie," her mother began. "Your sister explained everything to me, and I want it on record that I was dead set against it; we both could have gotten hurt—or worse. I drove my car around the corner to Willa Finch's house and left Angus with her. I walked back and sat here in the den in the pitch-black darkness for almost two hours. It was dreadful. All I could hear were my own thoughts about what might happen to us both." She tried her tea again, taking a quick sip with a satisfied smile.

"When Effie came in through the back door, Elle had asked me to text Detective Tanner and let him know what she was doing. I couldn't just wait there in the dark, so I followed her upstairs and let her talk. I was worried that the police wouldn't arrive in time, so I did what any good mother would do."

"That leads me to the second part of that question," Lana said. "Mama, you really held her at gunpoint until Jonah got there?"

"You're damn right I did," she replied with an expression of triumph. For a moment, Elle imagined that her mother sat a little taller and looked ten years younger.

"Language, Mama," Elle chided. Vee ignored her.

"Baby girl, what was all that with our trip to the library?"

Elle sat up and stretched. She moved Angus into her lap and stroked the dog's enormous ears.

"There was a piece missing to all this," she explained. "Grady's picture had three girls, and someone had gone to the trouble of taking it from Duncan's body. I didn't know if it was a third victim, or someone involved on the other end. I needed to find out who she was."

"Why the library trip?"

"It was something Dan said about his mother. He actually used the word *quamished* when talking about her. It was something she had said on his wedding day. That got me thinking about some of the conversations I had had with Peg and Effie. They both used several colloquialisms and phrases I hadn't heard for years."

"You lost me," her sister admitted.

"Words like *quamished*, *mommucked*, and *pizer* and some of their past-tense phrasings are only found together in an old dialect from up around the Wanchese and Ocracoke areas. The locals call it High Tider, or more often Hoi Toider, because of the way the *o* is elongated. It's actually got some roots in Middle English and Scottish English."

"Lana, do you remember your papa's friends Elaine and Jed?" her mother asked. "They were from Harkers Island and had that same kind of accent." Lana shrugged.

"I had never thought about that connection before, until I started looking for one. It wasn't much to go on, but it gave me a nudge that Effie might be part of this. Then, if you look at the picture, the girls are sitting in front of a lighthouse. It didn't take long to identify it as the Cape Lookout Lighthouse; it's just south of Pamlico Sound. Those black and white diamonds are a dead giveaway. At least I knew I was on the right track."

"What did Rosa dig up for you?" Lana asked.

"I was hoping to find something more solid than a guess. I knew we could probably connect Shona and Peg. Dan also mentioned that Shona's parents had died in an accident when she was young. Peg's maiden name, assuming she was telling the truth, was Garrish, which is an old Ocracoke family name."

Lana shook her head. "That's still a needle in a haystack."

"Those were Rosa's exact words," Elle agreed. "And with privacy laws, I won't have access to most of those census records for another several years. Still, I had a last name and a general idea of a time frame. The only problem was that most of these small-town papers don't have digital archives. In a lot of cases, there aren't even paper copies available.

"Rosa and a colleague in Hyde County went through several years of manual copies of the local papers. She worked her magic and came up with an article about a house fire that killed a married couple about that same time. The family's name was Garrish. The fire made for big news at the time. Three children were listed as survivors, and the oldest was sixteen."

"The three you were hoping for?" Lana asked.

"I wasn't entirely sure," Elle replied. "No names were given, but Rosa found a microfiche record of the matching obituary that listed the three surviving girls: Seonag, Maighread, and Oighrig. All three are good, old-world names."

"I think I see where this is going," Lana commented.

Elle nodded. "It was all the confirmation I needed. Seonag softened into Shona, which is a common diminutive. Maighread is a less common spelling of Margaret, which becomes Maggie, Meg, Peg, or even Daisy. Finally, Oighrig traditionally shortens to Effie, even though the two names have totally different etymological origins." As she spoke, her mother nodded with pride.

"Now that I was sure the three were sisters, the link to Kirk & the Tartans made sense. Effie and Peg were bleeding it dry, with or without Shona's help."

"What happened to poor Kirk makes more sense, too," Lana added. "First, their parents die in a house fire, then Kirk dies in a bar fire. Makes you think."

Vee set her empty teacup on the coffee table and looked from one daughter to the other. "It just makes me think how sad this all is. Nothing but naked greed, really, destroyed how many lives? How many families?" She took a daughter's hand in each of hers and squeezed. "It makes me appreciate what we have."

Epilogue

A low, stone and iron lattice wall surrounded the courtyard at St. Columba's Church on the western edge of St. Andrews. Just beyond an arch of metal and night blooming jasmine, a small group congregated in the parish graveyard. In the early morning hour, a priest was offering burial rites as the participants looked on.

Elle stood along the small open grave, flanked on one side by her mother and sister and by Dan and Paige on the other. Angela, Mrs. Scott's caregiver, stood along the other side with Jonah Tanner and Jeannie Pace.

"God of comfort, let your presence be known to each who suffers from this loss. Let them know freedom from pain, freedom from grief, and freedom from despair. Amen."

As the congregants repeated the Amen in unison, a pair of church sextants lowered the small cedar box of ashes into the ground. They began to fill the hole with dirt as the group departed to the courtyard.

Angela gave each of them a hug, stopping for a moment to talk to Elle.

"I'm glad you could come this morning," Elle said.

"I never met Duncan, but I know Mrs. Scott would have wanted to be represented. Somewhere in her soul, I am sure she is at peace now." She hugged Elle a second time and returned to her car.

As the group dispersed, Dan and Elle lingered under the jasmine-covered trellis. She could tell he had been crying, but she sensed it was grief leaving his body. They stood for a few moments in silence.

"Your mother didn't have to do this, Elle," he began.

"She's had this plot for decades," she replied. "Lately, though, she's made it clear she has no intention of spending eternity in a box underground. She wants to be scattered across St. Andrews and back home in Scotland. She decided this was a better use for the spot. Duncan lost years of his life for something that was never his fault, so she felt this was the least she could do."

Through the short service, Dan had seemed distracted, his face wan and colorless. It couldn't be easy trying to come to terms with everything that had happened, Elle thought. "How are you doing, Dan? Really?"

He shrugged. "I'm a pile of mixed emotions right now. I'm glad that everything came to light—there's no doubt of that. At the same time, I'm trying to understand my mother's role in all of this. More than anything, I'm working hard to let go of years' worth of anger. It's not easy."

She wrapped an arm around his shoulders and pulled his cheek in for a brief kiss. "You're doing exactly what you need to do. And I'm here if you need to talk."

"I appreciate it, Ellie. Even when I'm wallowing in feeling sorry for myself, I think about Duncan. He was just a normal kid, doing his best. They took everything away from him. His entire life was gone in a flash. He spent five years locked up, and he probably never understood why."

OFF SCOT FREE

She nodded and squeezed his shoulder. "We have done what we can to right the wrong that was done to him. Now, it's our turn to let that grief go. Like Mama always says, 'You'll never be free as long as you're chained to where you've been.'"

As she spoke, she looked back to the sextants hard at work in the church's yard. She hoped Duncan was finally free.

ABOUT THE AUTHOR

A lifelong lover of the great authors and sleuths of detective fiction's Golden Age, William Ashe grew up on the twisty tales of Agatha Christie, Ngaio Marsh, John Dickson Carr, Ellery Queen, and other mystery masters. Few things pique his interest more than an old book filled with secluded county estates, shady heirs, locked rooms, and impossible murders.

Liam's inaugural series, featuring professional researcher and Scottish historian Elle Cunningham Mackay, is an homage to these masters—with a little modern sensibility mixed in. Elle's Scottish-flavored mysteries will immerse the reader in a work of kilts, bagpipes, Highland games and haggis.

Liam's other titles include the Arca Noctis series of thrillers starring curiosity store owner Emery Vaughn and a pair of Golden Age series featuring former spy Mafalda Marchand and village vicar James Valentine.

Love classic mysteries? Visit www.liamashe.com and sign up for Liam's free, monthly email newsletter. You'll receive updates about Elle's newest titles and special ebook offers on his latest mystery and thriller series.

Made in the USA
Columbia, SC
27 September 2023